DANIEL COLDSTAR

THE RELIC WAR

Also by Stel Pavlou

Daniel Coldstar: The Betrayer

THE RELIC WAR

STEL PAVLOU

An Imprint of HarperCollinsPublishers

Daniel Coldstar #1: The Relic War

 For information address HarperCollins Children's Books, a division of HarperCollins Publishers, 195 Broadway, New York, NY 10007.

www.harpercollinschildrens.com

Library of Congress Control Number: 2017943445

ISBN 978-0-06-212606-1

Typography by Joel Tippie

19 20 21 22 23 PC/BRR 10 9 8 7 6 5 4 3 2

❖

First paperback edition, 2019

For Michelle

CONTENTS

Somewhen in the Exodussic Age . . .

1
THE DISAPPEARED

There is a burn mark where Daniel Coldstar used to sleep.

They took him in the middle of the night. They came while he slept, pulled him from his bed, and only fired their weapons when he put up a fight. The other children heard him screaming, heard the flap of wings retreat into the night. And then nothing.

Silence.

He was gone.

A week later and it was the same for Dathan Tantus. A few days after that it was Kree Kalamath's turn, though he didn't even make it into his bunk before they got him.

That was how it was in the Racks. Here one minute, gone the next. The empty beds a reminder of who once had been and were no more.

Twenty or so children each shared a Rack, bunk beds that towered up out of the bedrock like rusted nails, standing a hundred deep in every direction. They called themselves grubs, clinging to their beds like fleas, as though threadbare blankets were any kind of refuge from the mines; especially at night, when *they* came, scuttling across the walls, metal talons digging into the stone.

Clickity-click . . . clickity-click . . . clickity-click . . .

The Nightwatchers–a terrible mix of dead machine and living insect–if insects grew to the size of a man. They scanned the city of rust each night, probing the darkness in search of their next target. Some made a kind of mechanical groan, as though trying to lay an egg. Others swooped across the Racks, the beat of their wings counting down to the moment of attack.

And yet the Nightwatchers weren't even the worst part. Next came a LightEye, a purely robotic creation with more legs than its stunted processor knew how to handle. Its armored body raised up off the ground as though afraid of getting its pretty dress wet, until *snap*–

It seared the Racks with the light of a miniature sun.

And all this happened before the arrival of the true demons of the mines, the Overseers–who marched into the Racks wrapped in the stench of oil and decay. They were the shape of men, but they were not men. Their arms were too thin, their bodies too misshapen, and their weather-beaten masks with eyes too far apart and too numerous to possibly belong to a person–these were who the Nightwatchers looked to for their orders. These were who the grubs truly feared.

They always came in a troop, usually around ten or so with a commander at the front. Rust weeping from their armor, the Overseers stood in silence and watched.

Overhead, the Nightwatchers circled, air whooshing through their tattered wings, waiting for the signal from the Overseers–the hammer end of a lone blast-pike striking the ground in one almighty punch–urging them to snatch whichever child they had chosen.

As a grub, there was nothing you could do but pray that they hadn't come for you.

Except on this night, something changed.

An Overseer pounded his blast-pike into the ground, not once, but twice.

The grubs listened to the scuffle of feet, but no one dared look down from their bunk until one of the Overseers spoke. The words projecting from his helmet were a terrible, artificial-sounding version of common Koin, the galaxy-wide language all the grubs understood, even if some of them couldn't actually speak it. It was nothing like the Overseer's true voice, a gibbering, grunting kind of noise, muffled beneath his helmet. The Overseer said, "Forty-one eighty-two, get moving!"

Prodded into the open, a single boy stumbled out from

behind the line of Overseers and into the light cast by the LightEye.

Audible gasps echoed between the Racks, followed by frantic whispers in Jarabic and Chaff and a hundred other languages as the grubs tried to understand what was happening.

The boy wobbled on unsteady legs, trying to get his bearings, as one Rack after another became a pillar of faces peering down at him. Faces he didn't know, but who clearly knew him.

Impatient, another Overseer swung his blast-pike at the boy's head–

"Dee!" a voice cried from the shadows.

A few Racks away, a lone grub with pale eyes clambered down from his bunk as fast as he could, jumping the final few rungs to the ground.

Barreling into the light, he pulled up short when he saw the boy flinch at his approach–

Ssssnappp!

"No!" the returned boy cried, rocking on his heels.

Too late! A tendril of electricity lanced out from the tip of an Overseer's blast-pike, smacking the grub across the Racks. He landed in a cloud of dust at the boy's feet.

The Racks fell silent.

The commander of the troop signaled the Overseers to move on. With the LightEye clumsily tagging along behind, they marched out, leaving the two boys to get acquainted.

"Dee . . . ?" the grub on the ground said, clearly in pain, and not caring one bit. "Dee, it's me, Blink."

The name meant nothing to the boy Blink called "Dee."

Blink hauled himself up. "Daniel Coldstar," he said, shaking his head. "I can't believe you're back."

4182

"What do you want?" said Daniel, not sure who he should trust.

What did any of them want? Who were these people? He backed up, looking for a way out, his hands shaking.

Blink looked at him, as if to say, *Isn't it obvious?* "I want to know where you've been," he replied.

"Is that a trick question?"

"Trick question? What are you talking about? Dee, you've been gone almost a month! Where were you?"

"I don't know!" Daniel barked. Show no fear, he kept telling himself. Show no fear. He balled his quivering hands into fists, pretended like his heart wasn't trying to beat its way out of his chest. "Who are you?" he demanded. "Do I know you?"

Blink rocked on his heels. "Know me?" he said. "What did they do to you?"

"How come you're still alive?" another voice demanded from somewhere high up in the Racks.

Daniel glanced over his shoulder. Grubs from all over were venturing down from their bunks to gawk, crowding in, their stench making it difficult to breathe. Some sharp-nosed kid got right in his face, screaming in God knows what language.

A grub, with dirty fingernails growing out of his scalp where his hair should have been, did the translating. "Fix is right, nobody ever comes back. Never."

Daniel looked around. "And coming back here is a good thing?"

"What makes you so special?" someone else asked.

"Maybe he knows the way out," said another desperately.

"Know the way out?" This was getting out of hand. "I don't even know where I am. I don't know who you are." Fire ripped through Daniel's veins. "I don't know who any of you are!"

"Keep the noise down!" the kid with the fingernail hair pleaded. "They'll hear us."

Daniel didn't care; all he knew was that if this kid got any closer, he was going to slug him. "Back off!"

Some of the grubs did as they were told. Others appeared baffled. The grub called Blink stood his ground. "Dee," he said, "it's just us."

"Same goes for you too," Daniel warned.

That seemed to quiet them down like nothing else, which threw Daniel because he couldn't get a read on why. "Are you their leader?"

"Wow," one of the kids in back said. "He sure got socked in the socket."

"Blink Darkada is your best friend," said the kid with the fingernail hair. "At least, he was."

"He still is," Blink replied, taking a step forward, trying not to flinch.

Daniel kept his fist ready, just in case. "What happened to your eyes?" he asked.

Blink's eyes were a greenish blue, with no sign of a pupil.

"He's from one of the Burn Worlds," another kid said.

"He can stare at a sun without blinking," Fingernails explained. "Doesn't even go blind."

"Fat lot of use it is down here," said the first kid.

"I *might be* from the Burn Worlds," Blink corrected, annoyed. "It's just a guess."

"You don't know where you're from?" asked Daniel.

Blink almost smiled. Almost. "None of us know where we're from, Dee."

Daniel glanced around at the leather-faced grubs as if seeing them for the first time. They were just kids, looking as lost as he felt, hoping he had a pocketful of answers. Daniel let his fist relax. "I'm sorry," he said.

"What are you sorry for?" one of the grubs said. He had

skin like tree bark, but when he held out his hand to Daniel, the warmth in that simple gesture felt like home. "They really wiped your brain clean, didn't they? Maybe you'll remember more tomorrow." He introduced himself as Dakan Liss, though most called him Choky, he explained.

Daniel hadn't even finished shaking his hand when the other grubs, wanting to do the same, unleashed a torrent of names he'd never remember. Fix Suncharge patted him on the back, Henegan Rann, that mute kid Gungy Wamp, and Ogle Kog, who came from some world with super-high gravity, so he was shorter than most, but he claimed he could jump to the top of a Rack in one bound–Daniel wasn't sure why that was important, but whatever.

"What about you?" Daniel asked, turning to the kid with the fingernail hair. "What's your name?"

"Name's Matthew Fleet," he said. "We dug out the Worm together, before the cave-in."

None of that seemed familiar to Daniel.

"You used to call me Nails?"

Daniel shrugged. "Okay . . ."

But before he could ask any more . . . "WHO DISTURBS–?" a Nightwatcher yawped from on high.

The cry echoed from one side of the Racks to other. Startled, the grubs froze. "Who disturbs?" cried another Nightwatcher a little farther away. "Who disturbs?"

It was too dark to see them, but the grubs could certainly hear the wretched creatures stretch out their wings, readying for the hunt. Either the Nightwatchers had returned or they had never left, but the grubs were so excited by Daniel's return, few noticed. The time for talking was over. One more call from a Nightwatcher, and there were no prizes for guessing what came next.

"Go!" Blink whispered.

They scattered to the four corners of the Racks like vermin avoiding the light, clambering up ladders or over one another to get back to their bunks.

"Where do I sleep?" Daniel asked, hurriedly.

"That one over there," Blink said, quickly pointing it out. "Top bunk."

Daniel took a breath. "Thanks," he said.

Blink nodded. The two boys eyed each other, a moment of understanding before going their separate ways. Blink fled into the darkness. Daniel ran the other way, Nightwatchers swooping over his head. He gripped the rungs to his Rack, the rust cutting into his hands, and climbed as fast as he could on legs that had little strength. His whole body shook with the effort. Every time he took a step, he worried less about the Nightwatchers and more about plunging to his–

No more rungs!

Daniel pitched forward into the charred remains of a blanket sprawled across a long, abandoned bed. The pillow, if you could call it that, smelled like something had been living in it. There were deep scratch marks all over the frame where something violent had happened.

"I'm starting to think disappearing was the better option," he said to no one in particular.

It was the perfect thing to do to draw attention to himself. A Nightwatcher dove right in, its gigantic wings outspread. It landed at the foot of Daniel's bunk with a clank, its clawed mechanical feet curling tightly around the rail, leaving fresh, deep grooves in the metal.

"Who disturbs?" the Nightwatcher demanded.

Daniel so badly wanted to answer back, but he knew it would probably be the biggest mistake he could make. This thing towered over him. He didn't stand a chance.

Instead, he rolled over and pretended to be asleep, while the Nightwatcher sat at the end of his bed, cocked its head, and watched him.

A HAMMERTAIL NEVER FORGETS

The TRS-80 GoLoader had three massive headlights mounted in front, and a mile-long train of mine cars behind it. Beneath its rusted-out shell sat a grease-smeared guidance system broadcasting a steady stream of orders to every mine car within a ten-mile radius, instructing them to either join the train or detach and head elsewhere. Sitting on a string of antigravity repulsers, the entire contraption didn't care about tracks, road, or terrain–it flew through the mines, its blackened attitude adjusters flipping the vehicle onto its side, or rolling it completely over every time it accelerated into a bend.

Daniel, his fingers curled around the bars of the cage on one of the mine cars, drank in the damp air of the mine shaft. What was that smell? A kind of spicy aroma that made his stomach growl; there was something so . . . familiar about it.

"I'd stand back if I were you," Blink warned.

The other grubs in the mine car were already backing away, but Daniel was more interested in what he saw down the tunnel, a tangled forest of bone-white roots hanging from the tunnel wall.

"I don't think we're going to get through," he said.

But he was wrong. The GoLoader hurtled toward the obstruction, while the fleshy limbs recoiled from its lights. They were more animal than vegetable.

Blink grabbed Daniel by the scruff and yanked him back right as the rattletrap plowed on through.

Bullets of severed tentacles exploded through the mine car, sawn off by the cage bars. They thrashed about on the deck for the longest time.

Blink held Daniel back. "Just wait," he said, "before you do anything else stupid." He explained that this was what the roots always did before dying.

The pale chunks of organic matter shook one last time before oozing with sticky sap.

Daniel shook him off. "What are they?"

"Breakfast," said Nails with a grin, scooping up a piece and taking one almighty bite.

It was every grub for himself, stuffing his pockets. As a food source, it didn't look very appetizing, but there was that smell again–spice.

Daniel nibbled on a piece. It was rough on his tongue, not nearly as slimy as it looked, and sweeter than he was expecting. It had him scrambling to fill his own pockets before it was all gone.

Passava . . . ? Was that the name of this stuff? Yes, Passava! The flood of relief at finally being able to latch on to a memory! If only it would lead to more, but Daniel had already started to realize that there was something very strange about the way his mind had been wiped clean. He could remember some things with perfect clarity, like language and numbers, but other things were completely missing, no matter how hard he looked. It was as though his mind knew that a memory was supposed to be in a certain compartment, but whenever he opened it all he found was an outline in dust of where it used to sit. The memory wasn't blocked; it had been taken, lifted out of his mind with precision, leaving a whole lot of nothingness.

Light flooded in through the bars of the mine car; the deathly glow of LightEyes spilling across ancient columns of carved stone, and around the ruins of once-mighty buildings.

"Where are they taking us?" Daniel asked between chews. He drifted back to the bars, watching an entire colony of grubs below crawl all over the ruins under the unforgiving watch of Overseers.

"Looks like the Snake," said Choky.

The Worm? The Snake? "Do any of these places have friendly names?"

"Why?" said Blink, joining him at the bars and sucking on a big piece of Passava. "Would it make you feel better?"

As the GoLoader dove down into a cavernous chamber filled with the deafening racket of crushers and motors, the overwhelming stench of fresh dung filled their nostrils. The staging post, where all snake-mining activity began and ended, was lined with animal pens as far as the eye could see, each enclosure crammed with trabasaurs of every conceivable size and type, from two-legged Ridgebacks with their razor-sharp teeth being saddled up and ridden out, to braying Chainhogs and Hammertails pulling smaller empty mine cars called skids down into the tunnels.

Trabasaurs! The surge of recognition turned Daniel's heartbeat into a drum. Just like the Passava, he recognized these too. Genetically engineered to resemble ancient dinosaurs, trabasaurs were the workhorses that required very little food and had allowed humans to colonize the galaxy. . . .

What the heck was a dinosaur?

So many gaps in his memory. This was going to be frustrating.

Descending to ground level, the GoLoader lurched to a stop before throwing open its gates. Daniel stepped out into a sea of a thousand boys from a hundred worlds making their way toward the Overseer checkpoints.

Swept along with everyone else, Daniel picked his way around the remnants of a statue, now a jigsaw puzzle in stone. It had more arms and legs than any person, with an utterly alien face.

"Who were they?" Daniel wondered.

"How should I know?" said Blink, hurrying over to snag a place in line close to one of the hot-steam vents. "I don't even know who I am."

"What do you think happened to them?"

"I don't care," Blink replied, sounding annoyed. "You used to feel the same way."

"I did?" That didn't seem right. Sure, he had a tough time remembering his life before yesterday, but he still knew who he was deep down inside. His gut was very clear; he wanted answers. "What are they having us dig for, anyway?"

Blink couldn't hide his disappointment. "You really don't remember a thing, do you? Sheesh, you're a lot of work."

Daniel shrugged. "Help me out."

"This is a relic mine," Nails chimed in. "Whatever this civilization once had, the Overseers want it–"

"Oh, remember that thing!" Choky blurted with a wheezing laugh. "What was that thing?"

Blink took another Passava root out and started chewing on it. "I don't know, some giant freaking robot. Took us days to chisel it out. What was it, like a million years old?"

Nails nodded and chimed in. "It still had power."

"As soon as it was free," Blink added, "it grabbed the guards, threw 'em down the chute, and tore off into next week."

"Did they ever catch it?"

Blink shrugged. "I don't know. I hope not. I'd like to think something made it out of here. It's not like anyone's ever coming to get us . . ."

They were near the front of the line now. Grimy, worn-out tool belts hung on hooks and the grubs each grabbed one. Daniel followed what everyone else did.

"Keep it fastened tight," said Choky. "It'll keep you alive if things go bad."

Daniel checked out the pouches, but everyone was watching him so closely, he didn't even have to ask. The other grubs knew how confused he was.

"That's your water skin," Nails explained. "Don't forget to fill it up. Sometimes they forget to let us drink."

"What about this?" Daniel asked, pulling out a small, notched, cylindrical device.

Blink was right behind him. He grabbed it and stuffed it back into the pouch. "It's your Regulator. If you get in trouble, press it into your socket to activate–"

Socket? What the heck was his socket? What was Blink talking about? "What happens when I activate it?"

Blink nodded in the direction of the waiting Overseers. "They give us your coordinates and send us out to retrieve you. So don't lose it."

One of the other grubs tapped Daniel on the shoulder. No more talk–he was at the front of the line now and Overseers weren't known for their patience.

Daniel's heart did its best to hammer its way out of his chest. One more good thump and it would probably succeed.

He hung his head and forced himself to walk over to the checkpoint, trying not to pay attention to the heat radiating from the blast-pike in the Overseer's corroded hand. Electricity danced brightly at its tip, eager to find a target.

"Good morning, forty-one eighty-two," the Overseer said in that peculiar artificial rendering of Koin. "Your efforts in the relic war will be rewarded."

Daniel doubted that, especially when the animalistic grunting of the Overseer's true voice under the helmet sounded so unfriendly.

Daniel looked away, trying to ignore the putrid stink wafting out from beneath the Overseer's armor plates.

At twice his size, the Overseer loomed over Daniel and aimed a spindly finger at his head. He wanted to run, but he found himself bolted to the ground.

A tingling sensation shot up his ear. He held his hand up to try to stop it, only to find his skin peeling back. There was a small socket embedded in his temple.

Daniel's eyes flared wide, his mind jolted with detailed information and key skills–everything he would need to know to do his job today.

When it was over, Daniel jerked his head back. "Hey! Did you just put your finger in my head?" He reached up, feeling around the strange object embedded in his skull. It itched like crazy.

The Overseer jabbed him to get moving.

Daniel held up his hands and backed away through the checkpoint. By the time he turned back around, it was the weirdest thing: all of a sudden he knew where to go, and what to do, without question.

He glanced over at Blink, jerking a thumb at the trabasaur enclosures, like he'd done it a million times before.

Who knows, maybe he had?

In the first corral, a crash of massive Hammertails waited impatiently for their troughs to be filled. On the far side, a few grubs had separated one animal into a pen and were busy pulling a harness over its tough, gray folds of skin. He was about the size and shape of a rhinoceros, but his horns weren't on his nose; they were clustered around a massive club tail that swayed menacingly from side to side.

"Watch it. He's in a mood," one of the grubs warned.

Daniel reached up and ran a hand softly over the animal's neck, careful to avoid the stains of oil seeping from the glands on each side of the beast's head. That stuff never came off.

Weird, he knew how to handle a Hammertail. . . . He hadn't remembered any of this until just a moment ago. What other information had the Overseer injected into his brain?

The beast fidgeted, stomping his front pads on the ground. He was trying to glance back, but his neck hadn't evolved that way and there was no room in the pen to turn around. He snorted, hot steam blowing from his nostrils.

"Easy, eeeeasy . . ." Daniel said, trying to sound as calm and reassuring as he could.

He wasn't afraid, even when the animal reared up and could easily have crushed him. Why wasn't he afraid? He slid around to the front so they could look each other right in the eye.

It was a moment Daniel hoped he would never forget for the rest of his life. He peered into the dark brown eye of this magnificent, enormous beast, and saw a deep friendship staring back. This Hammertail knew him.

The animal immediately calmed, purring in deep, rumbling tones. He bowed his head and nuzzled against Daniel's chest.

"I see Alice remembers you," a boy in the next pen commented. Unlike Daniel, he wore his dugs, the rugged pewter jumpsuits that all the grubs wore, fastened right up to his neck with the collar pulled up around his ears. He was riding a Ridgeback, but the once-proud animal was cowed and beaten. Dried blood had encrusted around puncture wounds in its side, right where the spikes on the boy's stirrups gleamed.

The boy introduced himself as Pinch. "These pathetic beasts are the only creatures allowed to remember anything around here. I understand Darkada and his friends have been trying to get you to remember what happened. Take my advice, don't try to remember," Pinch warned with disdain. "It's forbidden. It breeds ideas and ideas breed trouble. You'll just make it worse for yourself. You have a chance to start over. Don't waste it."

Pinch attempted a smile, clearly not something his face was used to. "Just my advice," he said, "unless you want to make a habit of disappearing."

Daniel kept his mouth shut. If he opened it now, things would probably get ugly.

The grubs opened the gates and Pinch jabbed his ride. The animal cried out in pain, dutifully whisking its master off down the nearest tunnel.

Alice started gnawing on Daniel's dugs. "Hey!"

Alice the Hammertail complained, and tried again.

Daniel reached into his pocket and pulled out a Passava root, holding it up so Alice couldn't get to it. "Is this what you're after?"

Alice lunged for it, but Daniel was quicker. He took the reins and clucked a couple of times. "C'mon, then," he said. "Behave yourself and you might get this."

The Hammertail snorted, happy to play along.

4

IT'S ALL FUN AND GAMES UNTIL SOMEBODY BRINGS A DROTE

If there was a worse place to be in than a relic mine, Daniel didn't know where it was, but at least now he knew why they called it the Snake.

A long, winding tunnel, its walls oozing with moisture, led down to a vaulted area of the mine they called the Workings, a cathedral of misery perfumed with the stench of rot. This was where the real mining happened. Grubs caked in mud were crammed onto excavation scaffolds, hammering and digging, loading up skids with rubble for trabasaurs to haul off.

Somewhere around the middle of the Workings, sandwiched between a rickety observation platform and some kind of pulverizer, Daniel found Blink holding an angry, snaggletoothed rodent by the scruff. He struggled to coax the mean-tempered ball of crazy into a bait-box, while Fix Suncharge steadily backed away, clutching his bloodied hand and ranting in Jarabic.

"Of course it'll bite; it's a drote!" Blink snapped, frustrated.

Fix wasn't nearly done complaining, but Blink was having none of it. "Forget it!" he said. "I'm doing it!"

"Making friends?" Daniel remarked.

Blink glanced up, panic punching him between the eyes. "Whoa! Whoa! Stay back!" he warned.

Fix scrambled to block Daniel's way.

"Alice gets one whiff of this drote and all hell breaks loose." Blink crammed the struggling drote's head into the bait-box. The creature kicked violently with its back legs, but Blink had the drop on it.

The bait-box snapped shut, trapping the raging drote inside.

Daniel, still giving Alice's muzzle a soothing rub, asked, "Are we good?"

Blink breathed easy. "While there's carbon between 'em, Hammertails could care less."

Daniel pretended he understood, but he really didn't. His incredibly brief socket education had given him the knowledge to wrangle Alice, but there were clearly still gaps in what he knew.

"Get moving!" an Overseer ordered. The guard towered over them on the observation platform, blast-pike aimed at the far side of the Workings. "Section Five."

Blink answered for all of them. "Yes, Master Overseer," he said, bowing his head.

The rock face at Section Five glowed like hot coals beneath the blazing LightEye. The markings daubed all over it were not in Koin, or any language Daniel recognized for that matter, but other sections had similar markings, so he got the gist. The Overseers had definite plans about where they wanted to mine next.

Daniel led the Hammertail into position. "This'd be a whole lot quicker if they just used machines," he said.

"But bruised flesh won't destroy their precious relics," Blink remarked. He opened up one of the pouches on his tool belt, pulled out a scent marker, and began dabbing its sticky contents over the marks left by the Overseers.

"What's that for?"

"Didn't they just fill your head with instructions on how to mine down here?"

"Kind of. I'm still trying to process it," Daniel confessed.

Fix nudged him out of the way, setting down a bait-box with a bucket of water not far from it. He seemed pleased with the setup.

Alice's ears twitched. He was thirsty.

Daniel led him over for a drink. The sixteen-ton beast nudged the bait-box out of the way as though claiming his territory, and thrust his huge mouth into the bucket.

"Just let him loose," said Blink, spotting a cohort of

Overseers approaching. "Come on, before they get any ideas."

Daniel unhitched the leash and the three boys ran. "Where are we going?"

Fix snapped at him in Jarabic.

"What did he say?"

"He said anywhere but here!"

Whatever the heck the sudden rush was all about, Daniel didn't know, but he knew enough not to question it at the moment.

Fix snatched a pebble up off the ground and lobbed it up at a bunch of squabbling grubs huddled on a gantry overlooking their section. It dinged on one of the metal uprights.

"Will you hurry up?" said Blink. "It's about to get busy down here."

A couple of grubs scrabbled around for a rusted-out ladder with a rung or two missing; it would have to do. The three boys climbed as fast as they could, pulling themselves up onto the gantry where the others were crowded around Henegan Rann, waving sticks of Passava in his scaly face. He was taking bets–

"Grubs!" he said. "This is Alice we're talking about. He whacks more guards than any other Hammertail in this entire miserable, stinking hole. You know he'll take out at least three of 'em–"

"I'm in," Blink said, pushing forward.

"Just the one?" Henegan took the stick of Passava and

tossed it into the bucket Ogle Kog was holding–

Wait, not a bucket. An Overseer's helmet–

Fix and Blink were arguing, but Henegan had other things to worry about. "You let me know what you decide," he said, turning to another kid. "No Passava, no bet. No exceptions!" He turned on Daniel. "What about you?"

Daniel hesitated. "What are the rules?"

Henegan shrugged; this was a no-brainer. "Simple. Guess how many Overseers Alice'll knock on their butts–exactly, mind you, not closest guess," he said, tapping the Overseer helmet in Kog's hand. "And the winner gets the whole stash."

"If there's more than one winner?"

"You split it."

"And if there's no winner?"

Henegan Rann flashed a smile. "Better luck next time," he said.

Henegan had obviously been running this thing for a while. He had a little more meat on his bones than most other grubs; beads and other odd little trinkets hung on strings around his neck, probably nothing important or the Overseers would never let him keep them. But he clearly made out like a bandit.

"What do you say?"

"No, I'm good," said Daniel.

"Suit yourself–"

Someone farther down the gantry gave a couple of

sharp taps on the metal handrail. The guards had finished inspecting the site and had settled on a target.

The mining process worked like this: Hammertails were strong enough to smash through solid rock, but sucked at taking orders. Hammertails hated drotes, so drotes were released to get them all riled up. The problem was drotes couldn't take orders either, but since drotes were wildly attracted to certain smells, the grubs used scent markers to get them to go where they wanted–which were the spots they needed the Hammertails to hit. A few good hits and the tunnels soon opened up a few more paces.

It sounded more complicated than it really was, and Daniel had no idea why the Overseers wanted to do it this way, but it worked.

While the rest of the troop watched from a safer vantage point, a lone Overseer took his blast-pike and pressed its electrified tip against one of the marks Blink had left on the wall. The substance began to smoke.

Ogle Kog put his hand over the helmet, muttering something in Chaff.

Henegan held up his hands. "No more bets," he said, happily sitting down and swinging his legs over the edge to watch the show–the smoke, curling down the rock face, creeping along the ground, and smothering the bait-box until–*click*.

A series of vents opened up all around the box.

The drote sensed the sickly, sweet odor almost

immediately, drawing it into a state of frenzy. Sharp claws probed the vents, scratching for a way out.

Alice flattened his ears back.

"Ladies, if there's one thing a Hammertail hates," said Henegan, with relish, "it's an odious drote–"

"Let's hope he hates it enough to smash us a way out of here . . ." Blink said, leaning against the railing.

Daniel glanced over at him. Now he understood the strange look Blink had had in his eye when Daniel came back. Underneath the joy of seeing a friend who had survived was the pain of shredded hope that Daniel had gotten out–but maybe there really was no escape from this place.

The bait-box snapped open and the drote poked its head out. Alice bellowed at it, thick globs of spit spraying from his mouth.

The drote paid no attention. It ventured out into the open, intent on finding where the aroma was coming from–then darted between the Hammertail's legs.

Alice jumped around in circles trying to stamp the drote into oblivion, but the drote was quicker. Letting out a shrill screech, it shot across the rocky ground and clawed its way up the rock face, following the train of smoke to–

Smash!

The massive ball of spikes at the end of Alice's tail clubbed the mine wall, peppering the chamber with shards of rock–

Smash!

The drote jumped for cover.

Smash! Smash!

The ground shook as Alice padded around, raging, swinging his horn-crested tail into the rock face, again and again, until–

The entire roof of Section Five collapsed down on the Hammertail in a tremendous column of rubble and dust, leaving the choking grubs gasping for air.

The Overseers stood impassively watching, untroubled by the chaos.

Henegan did a quick head count. "One, two . . . aw, bad luck, ladies. Not one Overseer with so much as a scratch? Banker wins. Better luck next time."

He got up to leave, urging Ogle Kog to bring the pot before someone started a fight.

Down below, an Overseer aimed the sparking tip of his blast-pike up at Daniel. "Forty-one eighty-two," he said. "Retrieve your animal."

Daniel bowed his head, just as Blink had done earlier, saying simply, "Yes, sir." He scrambled back down the ladder, while the Overseer turned on the other grubs.

"Back to work!"

Blink and the others quickly divided themselves up into teams, setting up a skid and passing the debris to each other in a chain like they had done a thousand times before. Alice had smashed out a whole new section of tunnel that extended at least ten paces deeper into the rock face than before, and the debris was considerable.

As for Alice, he didn't want to move.

Daniel jammed two fingers into his mouth and let out an earsplitting whistle.

Alice glanced nonchalantly over at him through the cloud of ancient dust. The enormous animal had taken up his repose on the far side of the heap of rubble, pleased with his work, but now quite tired from all the exertion.

"Are you going to lie there all day?"

One of Alice's ears twitched, as if to say that the thought had crossed his mind.

Daniel reached into his dugs and pulled out a root. "I have Passava," he said, waving it.

Alice's eyes lit up. Rolling awkwardly onto his feet, he shook the dirt from his body and sneezed.

"Bless you," Daniel said, without thinking. He tossed the root over, Alice catching it with one snap of his huge jaws.

Bless you . . . ?

The words came out naturally, but Daniel didn't recognize them. What did "bless you" even mean?

LIGHTS-OUT

Then it happened again.

A couple nights later, back in the Racks, Daniel rolled out a handful of multifaced dice across the dirt floor. At least, the grubs used them as dice; what they were actually used for was anyone's guess. Eight-sided, twelve-sided, tiny little shapes with markings on them, all a bunch of different colors and as old as the universe. Like all the other little knickknacks and oddities the grubs had found in the trash heaps of the mines, whatever the Overseers had deemed was of no value the grubs had taken for themselves and would trade in the hour the Overseers gave them each night before lights-out.

Daniel scored a three, a six, a triangle, and–well, who knew what that symbol was supposed to be. Point was, this was a winning throw–

"Aw, bad luck," Blink said, reaching out for the pieces.

Daniel batted his hand away. "Hey, those are mine. It's the same score you rolled ten minutes ago."

"When there was a nine in play. There's no nine in play now."

There wasn't a score anywhere in the dirt higher than his. How could he have lost? "You're just making these rules up as you go along," Daniel said, wiping his nose on his sleeve.

Blink tried to sound offended, but it was hard to do when all he did was laugh. "I'm not."

And that was when it was Daniel's turn to sneeze. Loud and dry, it echoed between the Racks—

Aaahhh-choooo!

"Bless you," said Blink, all matter-of-fact.

He wasn't alone: every grub within earshot said it, whether in common Koin or some other language, words that were like a gift from a time they were all forced to forget, rising up from the very bottom of their souls and given voice. It was strange, yet comforting and familiar all at once.

The room went quiet. Daniel and the other grubs eyed one another, hoping someone would remember the source of those words. Whoever each one had learned it from, their hearts quietly ached to be with them again. And for the longest time no one dared break the silence for fear that the warm sensation in their chests would disappear.

How could two words hold such power–for everyone–yet no one knew why? It didn't seem to matter what they looked like, what culture they belonged to, or what planet they came from; those two words bound them to each other. They told Daniel that he belonged. Just another forgetful kid, amid a thousand other forgetful kids, trying to figure out how to survive.

"Ah, this thing is a waste of time," Nails grumbled, getting up from the bottom bunk nearest to Blink. A mess of interconnected jagged pieces of some unknowable alien artifact jangled between his fingers; a puzzle defying a solution. "I'm either going to trade it or smash it into a thousand pieces. Who wants first dibs?"

"I'll smash it," Blink offered enthusiastically.

Nails rolled his eyes. "First dibs on trade," he said.

"What is it?" asked Daniel.

"How should I know?"

"It's alien poop," Choky explained, from up on one of the higher bunks. "It's what came out of their butts."

"You are disgusting," Nails shot back. "And you, Blink Darkada, need to stop taking advantage of Daniel just because he can't remember you're the biggest cheat in here." And with that, he stomped off.

Daniel glowered.

Blink gave a halfhearted shrug. "I'm sorry."

"No you're not."

"No. I'm not."

For the last few minutes before lights-out, the two boys sat propped up against one of the Racks listening to music. If you could call it that. Gungy Wamp had a whistle. Carved from a bone he'd pulled from a drote carcass way back when. It had four holes and couldn't hold a tune, but it was the sweetest sound anyone had ever heard. For a few minutes Mymon Ray joined in, drumming on his mess tin. A little kid, maybe six or seven, he beat that thing with such passion, Daniel couldn't help but smile, not because of any talent (he was terrible), but because of the pure joy on Mymon's face. In that moment Mymon Ray was free, and so was anyone listening.

6
DID SOMEBODY SAY DROTE?

"Good morning, forty-one eighty-two," said the Overseer, aiming his spindly finger at Daniel's head. "Your efforts in the war will be rewarded."

That tingling sensation shooting right into his head socket was nowhere near as disorienting now as it was the first time, but it still wasn't pleasant. Daniel glanced around the staging area while he waited for today's assignment to load into his mind. The usual thousand or so grubs marshaled the heavy machinery and livestock needed to work the mine as they always did. The chaos actually appeared to have some organization to it that made sense. Huh. He hadn't noticed that before. Come to think of it, had this Overseer taken a bath or was Daniel just getting used to the stink? Could you get used to something so bad so fast?

How long had he been back now anyways? Eight days? Nine?

Wait a minute. . . .

"Forty-one eighty-two, get moving. Your bait-box is waiting," the Overseer snapped. His real voice grunting underneath his helmet's electronic Koin sounded angrier and far more impatient than the translation suggested.

"I'm confused, sir," said Daniel hastily. "Normally I wrangle the Hammertails in the Snake–"

"Forty-one eighty-two, get moving. Your bait-box is waiting," the guard repeated, but this time the command was accompanied with the full force of his blast-pike.

Ssssnappp!

A sharp jolt of electricity surged into Daniel's wrist all the way up to his shoulder, leaving a smoldering burn mark on his dugs.

"Hey!" Daniel yelped, staggering back, rubbing his arm. "It was just a question–"

Blink, stepping out from his own reskill, grabbed Daniel by the same arm, marching him away from the checkpoint. "I will get him to his assignment, Master Overseer!" he called back over his shoulder.

Daniel shook him off. "Ouch!"

"Keep walking," Blink urged.

"I just asked a question. That's all I did."

"You don't ask them any questions, you just say 'Yes, sir' and do it. Haven't you figured that out by now?"

"They changed my job," Daniel explained as the two of

them made their way around the trabasaur pens. "I just got used to the last one."

"Job rotation, Dee," said Blink. "Happens every week." He put a finger to his head, swirling it around. "Keep us focused on how to perform instead of thinking about how to get out of here." He glanced back at the checkpoints, making sure the Overseers had forgotten all about Daniel's minor insubordination. "Just do what they say," he said, before pushing on into the crowd, leaving Daniel behind.

Daniel puffed out his cheeks, tension digging into his shoulders. Just when he thought he was getting the hang of this place.

"I hate drotes!" he called out.

Blink's arm rose up from the crowd, and with a simple wave he was gone.

A horn, deep and thrumming, blew from the far end of the staging post, followed by the deafening rumble of heavy machinery starting up. It wouldn't be long before it became so loud in here he'd be better off in the Workings.

Daniel pushed on, skirting around the far end of the corral, where the fence opened up and he could watch the bittersweet ritual of the trabasaurs being prepped for work—well, all except one, an irritable sixteen-ton Hammertail that was refusing to step into his harness.

Daniel leaned on the fence, trying to get Alice's attention with a couple of clucks.

Alice snorted, stomping his feet and refusing to turn around.

Acutely aware that the Overseers and the grubs over on the other side of the corral were watching his every move, Daniel signaled to them, *Let me try!* He lowered his voice. "Alice . . . what's going on?"

The animal shook his head from side to side, like he didn't want to listen.

Daniel rummaged around in his pockets for his breakfast. A fat, juicy Passava root, oozing with sap. He wafted it around, making sure Alice got a really good sniff of the thing.

Hesitantly Alice turned around, drool running down his mouth.

"You want it? Come and get it." Daniel held it out, waving it a couple of times. "Come on, you big lug!"

Alice snorted his disapproval again, loud and obnoxious, but he knew a good thing when he saw it. Slowly, he made his way over to Daniel, nuzzling before gently taking the root and chewing on it. Daniel ran his hand down the trabasaur's muzzle, giving him a good long look in the eye.

"Good boy," he said. "What's going on with you, huh?"

And then he saw them: bloody puncture wounds running in a line across Alice's ribs.

Daniel winced, rage swelling in his belly. "Who did this to you–?"

"Get away from my Hammertail!" Pinch Servilles demanded, marching across the corral, a barbed whip in his hand. "I have work to do."

"He's hurt," said Daniel, the anger rising in his throat.

He watched the boy approach, his dugs covered in mud, blood dripping from his spurs.

"He'll be more than hurt when I've finished with him," Pinch barked, raising his whip. "You've made him soft, Coldstar. Now it's up to me to teach this animal a lesson."

Without warning, Pinch swung his arm, striking Alice with a *snap!* The spurred end of the whip dug into the animal's flesh, only coming free when he yanked on it.

Alice cried out in pain, backing up a step or two.

"You didn't have to do that," Daniel said, the sound of quiet fury gripping his voice.

"Oh, go away, Coldstar, this has nothing to do with you."

"Touch him again," Daniel warned.

"Or what?"

In one bound, Daniel leapt over the fence, balling his fist, landing it straight in the other grub's face. Pinch dropped on the spot, blood dripping from a nasty split lip.

"Get up!" Daniel roared. "Come on!"

Pinch scrambled back, kicking up dirt, desperately trying to get away.

Daniel wasn't about to let him off that easy. Snatching the barbed whip up off the ground, he marched at the boy when–

Ssssnappp!

Several blast-pikes jabbed at his back, hurling him across the corral.

Barely able to see straight, Daniel flailed around in the dirt, unable to get up. Rolling onto his elbows, he clawed his way forward, only to find a pair of Overseer boots blocking his way.

"Put forty-one eighty-two in the pit," the Overseer said. "One cycle."

Daniel recognized his number right away. He began to panic. "The pit? What pit?"

Fearing for their own safety, a couple of grubs scrambled into action, dragging Daniel away by his ankles.

"What pit?" Daniel screamed. "Where are you taking me?!"

The gate to the corral creaked open, revealing that the entire staging post had ground to a halt to watch him. Silently, the sea of grubs parted for his journey toward an enormous rusty metal hatch sitting on the ground between the dung piles.

"What is that?" Daniel demanded, trying and failing to get a better look.

One of the Overseers pointed at it, triggering the lock. The hatch parted, two gigantic doors lifting up to reveal a deep hole dug into the bedrock.

Daniel struggled to break free, but it was useless. They threw him down into the pit with such force that when he landed the back of his head bounced off the ground.

Stunned, he gazed up at the grubs gathered around the hatch as they sealed him inside, but he couldn't make out any of their faces. The blow to the head had been so hard, all he could see were stars.

7
THE PIT

The first hour was the hardest.

Daniel had a sense of what an hour felt like when the lights were on, but here in absolute darkness time seemed to behave by a different set of rules. And his head . . . boy, it hurt.

He listened to the trabasaurs come and go, and the clank of Overseer boots marching overhead. He heard the distant voices of grubs doing as they were ordered.

At first he held on to the hope that they might change their mind and let him out, but that soon passed. Then he thought maybe he could find a way out of here; they hadn't taken his tool belt, after all, so maybe there was a chance. But a bumbling trip around the pit, scooting through the filth, seeing with his fingers, soon put an end to that idea.

He was alone with only his thoughts for company.

Daniel found a corner where he could rest and slid to the ground, hugging his knees. Maybe he was the lucky one? After all, there weren't any Overseers down here. Though the animal dung smelled pretty bad.

He closed his eyes, trying to relax. It didn't help. The same question kept rolling around in his brain: was it worth it?

Socking Pinch Servilles right in the jaw sure had made him feel a whole lot better, but it hadn't really changed anything. The Overseers didn't seem to care what that coward did to the animals.

Daniel sat slumped in the dark, with nothing to do but wait. . . .

"Ouch!"

Daniel had nodded off, slamming his head against the wall when he woke. How long had he been out?

He glanced up at the ceiling and toward the pit's only exit. Not that he could see it, but he could hear that something had changed. What happened to all the noise? The crushers had fallen silent. The heavy motors weren't rumbling. Where were the grubs? Nothing but a deathly silence hung over the staging post–

Slowly pulling himself to his feet, Daniel called out, "Hello?"

Nothing.

"Anyone there?" he asked, which was pointless because he knew there wasn't. They must have all gone back to the Racks for the night.

What the heck was he going to do now? There had to be some way to keep himself entertained.

He paced. He made up songs. He threw rocks at the walls, then threw rocks at the corners, getting them to skip back and forth between the walls a couple of times. He balanced rocks on his head. On his nose. He wasn't quite sure at what point he just sat there carving deep grooves into the ground, or when he had decided to turn around and start carving his name into the wall in huge letters, starting off with a triangular-shaped *D.* He could only guess at how spectacular it was going to look when he was finished.

Shhhwooooommmm . . .

What was that? The GoLoader! Were they coming back for him?

He jumped up. "Hey! Did you forget about me?"

Yes, yes! He could hear the trudge of a thousand pairs of boots disembarking. The grubs were back, but they were so noisy they were never going to hear him.

He lobbed a stone at the metal plate ceiling–

Dooonnnnggg!

Not bad. Sounded like a huge bell. He did it again.

Dooonnnnggg!

That should get their attention.

Dooonnnnggg!

A tiny hatch in the ceiling suddenly snapped back. Daniel stood directly under the light, but it was so bright he threw an arm over his eyes.

Staring down at him was an Overseer. "You will cease immediately," the Overseer commanded.

"Uhh . . . can I come out now?" Daniel pleaded.

The hatch snapped shut in response.

"Guess not . . ."

What he didn't expect was for the hatch to fly open again just moments later, and for a Passava root to come bouncing off his head.

He glanced up, his eyes still not fully adjusted, but he could tell just by the silhouette that this wasn't anybody that he knew. "Who's there? Who are you?"

"It's me," the figure whispered.

Great help. "Me who?"

"I thought you were gone," the figure said. "They said you were disappeared. I said more likely you'd escaped and were planning on rescuing us."

What was it about this person's voice that was so different from any of the other grubs? "Well, I'm back," said Daniel.

"Why are you in the dark?"

"Uhh . . . I like it?"

"Use your F-light!" the figure urged, pointing to the small device hanging from his belt.

Unsure what an F-light even was, Daniel carefully

unclipped it from his belt and warily pulled the trigger. A tiny orb no bigger than a bug shot up into the air, flared brightly, and began floating above his head.

Daniel rolled his eyes, frustrated. He could have done this hours ago!

The light was pretty weak, but it lit up the entire pit and, more importantly, let him see who it was he was talking to.

His mouth hung open when he did. "Wh . . . what are you?"

Was that confusion on the grub's face? He wasn't sure. "Did you just ask me what I am?"

"I'm sorry, they, er . . . did a wipe on me."

"A real good one too, by the looks of things," said the grub. "I'm a girl, you dumb lug."

A girl. With big, dark eyes and a way about her that was nothing like a boy. As the news that he'd lost his memory sank in, the confusion on her face gave way to hurt.

"Do you remember my name?"

Daniel shrugged. What could he say? "Sorry."

"I'm Nova," she said, utterly crushed. "Remember?"

Daniel shook his head.

She glanced back over her shoulder. "They're coming. Fourteen hours to go. You can do it, you always did."

And with that she snapped the hatch shut.

"Wait!" Now that he had some light, the bars running along the inside of the metal plates were visible. Just a short jump and he could hang on. Pulling himself up to the hatch, he pushed his head against it and peered out through the crack he'd managed to make.

In every direction there were grubs–and they were all girls.

"Holy drote . . ."

There had to be other Racks somewhere.

Daniel dropped back down to the ground, his heart racing, completely unable to process what he'd just learned. The mines were way bigger than he'd imagined. And there were . . . girls. Well, that just about blew his mind wide open.

As he spun around, lost in thought, his F-light spun with him, casting a glow over the entire back wall. There, under the pale, yellow light, Daniel saw his name carved into the stone. And next to it his name again. And again.

And again.

Twenty, thirty times. How many times had he written his name? How many times had he been here before?

"Gee," he said to no one in particular. "You'd think I'd know better."

When they did let him out, the girls were long gone and the boys had returned for a new day in the mine.

They marched him to the checkpoint, making it clear that there would be no rest. His day began now, just like everyone else's.

When it was his turn, Daniel stepped forward.

"Good morning, forty-one eighty-two," said the Overseer, his spindly finger delving into the socket in Daniel's head. "Your efforts in the war will be rewarded."

"No, no," said Daniel. "Your thanks is reward enough."

He'd taken barely a step when the blast-pike lit up the small of his back with a–

Ssssnappp!

"Get moving!"

This time Daniel held his tongue. So they'd wanted to teach him a lesson. Well, he'd learned a good lesson, all right. It just wasn't the lesson the Overseers had had in mind.

IN THE BELLY OF THE SNAKE

Section Five of the Snake had grown during Daniel's absence. Now it wormed its way fifty or more paces deep into the rock face, with massive fissures running throughout the tunnel head.

Blink and a gang of grubs were sorting through a heap of rubble looking for any sign of relics when Daniel arrived with his bait-box in hand.

Blink didn't look up from his work; he just said, "Sleep well?"

Setting the box down, Daniel just looked at him, only to realize that some grub he'd never seen before was already dabbing the gloopy end of a scent marker all over the wall at the end of the tunnel. "Hey!" Daniel called out.

The boy didn't respond.

"Hey!" Daniel said, marching over. "What do you think you're doing?" He grabbed the marker from the kid's hand.

The kid looked shocked. "I'm sorry!" he said. "I was just doing what they told me to do–"

"Well, don't. This gets screwed up, I'm the one going back in the hole."

The kid held up his hands and backed off. "I'm sorry."

Daniel shook his head, checking to see if the marker needed a refill on his way back to Blink. "Why didn't you tell me about Nova?" he said.

"And say what? I don't know her–you do. Anyway, how was I supposed to know if she's still alive? It's not like we get much contact with the other Racks."

"Who is she to me, anyway?"

Blink heaved another large rock onto the waiting skid and shrugged.

"I never talked about her?"

"Once or twice."

Daniel doubted that. Not with the way she acted. Something wasn't adding up.

"Eighteen seventy-three," an Overseer announced from back down the tunnel toward the Workings. "Vacate Section Five."

Blink bowed his head. "Yes, Master Overseer." He signaled to the rest of the gang to start heaving the skid full of rubble out of the tunnel. "You know," he said, turning to Daniel on his way out, "I don't got all the answers. Some of this you're going to have to figure out on your own. Take a look around, I got my own problems to deal with. We all do."

"I'm sorry," Daniel offered, watching him leave, a pang of guilt burning in his gut. Not because he had upset Blink, but because he suddenly realized that in one respect he had already been set free.

Whether by accident or by design, when the Overseers had wiped his mind, they had also deleted Daniel's memories of hopelessness. From his point of view everything was new again; he had no idea what was off-limits, because he had forgotten what those limits were.

But for Blink and everyone else it was different. Not only had they not forgotten what they had been through and what the consequences were, but they wore their despair like blinders.

If only Daniel could make them see the obvious, that life didn't have to be this way.

Daniel returned to his work with renewed purpose. Roughly, he began dabbing the scent marker all over the wall at the end of the tunnel. "There's got to be a way out of here," he muttered to himself. "There's got to be . . ."

Now that they'd filled his head with baiting techniques, maybe he could get Alice to smash them a way out of here.

He checked the bait-box, and it seemed to be in a pretty good spot. He peered inside to make sure the drote was awake. It spat at him.

"I hope he gets you good," said Daniel.

Taking one last look around, Daniel headed back up the tunnel, satisfied that everything was ready for an Overseer to come set the scent marker gloop on–

. . . fire.

The gloop was already burning. He could smell it–heck, the drote could smell it, ornery little dootbag. How was that even possible? He couldn't see any smoke coming from any of the marks he'd left on the wall. . . .

He glanced down at the scent marker in his hand. The one the boy had given him. It had been rigged to heat up. Smoking gloop was oozing out onto his glove.

"No, no, no, no, no . . ."

Too late. The smoke had already reached the bait-box, triggering the timer. That drote was jumping out in sixty seconds like it or not.

He had to warn them. He had to get down that tunnel and tell them to get that Hammertail out of here. Breaking into a run, sweat dripping off his face, Daniel raced down the passageway, only to find Pinch Servilles with Alice around the next bend.

"Oh dear," Pinch said, pretending to be shocked. "Something wrong with your equipment? How did that happen . . . ?"

With a smirk, Pinch held up Alice's leash.

"No, wait!" Daniel pleaded.

Too late. Alice was already loose–

Click!

The bait-box had opened!

Daniel threw up his hands. "Alice–stay! Staayy! Alice . . . ?" Daniel may as well have been talking to himself.

The animal's nostrils flared. He knew fresh drote when he smelled it. With his ears flattened, Alice pawed, then ground–and charged–

"No!" Daniel cried, backing up. "Bad boy! Noooo . . . !"

Yeah. Waste of time.

Daniel flipped around, running back the way he had come, down the tunnel and toward a dead end. There had to be somewhere he could hide–

Drote! Scrambling up his leg, trying to reach the smoking scent marker he still had clenched in his fist. Dropping the marker, he struggled to rip his drote-wrangler glove off while the creature hung on for dear life, licking at the smoking gloop–

There! He flung the glove over his shoulder, the drote leaping after it.

Behind him, back down the tunnel, he heard the first Alice-sized *smash!*

Then another. Closer this time.

Smash! Smash!

And before he knew it, he was out of tunnel.

With nowhere to go and nowhere to hide, Daniel watched helplessly as the two animals duked it out in what should have been the most lopsided fight ever. Except–Alice couldn't turn around–

The drote ran up one wall, onto the ceiling, leaping over the Hammertail's back, smoking scent marker hanging from its mouth, and all Alice could do was flick his tail. His natural instinct to spin around and really wind up for a strike had been completely taken away from him. He slammed one shoulder into the wall in one direction, then tried it again in the other, but nothing worked.

And boy, did the drote know it. Sitting just a couple of paces behind Alice, just out of reach of his clubbed tail, the scrawny little rodent licked the scent marker feverishly, safe in the knowledge that he was untouchable.

Alice, his massive face just inches from Daniel's, snorted in disgust. Daniel watched him pawing the ground. He watched the animal's mind ticking over until–he knew that look.

"Don't do it," Daniel begged. "Come on, Alice, I got thrown in the hole for you."

Whether Alice understood a word Daniel was saying made no difference now; Alice had already made his mind up. His tail really had freedom of movement in only one direction and he was happy to take advantage of it. With one almighty flex, Alice used his entire body to thrash his tail up and down, smashing the tunnel roof into oblivion–

Rubble rained down on the drote, followed by boulders so big it would be a miracle if the creature survived.

Crraaaackkkkk!

The fissures crisscrossing the tunnel head began expanding until the entire section began to cave in–

Daniel dropped to his knees, shielding himself with

his arms, his mouth filling with dust. He couldn't see, he couldn't breathe–

And then the most extraordinary thing happened.

Alice nipped at Daniel's dugs, pulling the boy under his chin for protection as though he were his calf, pushing the flat of his head up against the wall so that his entire body became one enormous shield while boulders rained down on his back for what felt like an eternity. . . .

When the chaos subsided, Alice strained to get back up on his feet, his grunts and snorts growing ever more desperate with each lunge. But the Hammertail would not quit, even as Daniel gasped for air, until he shook off their temporary tomb, emerging into a far larger tunnel head than had been there before.

Pulling Daniel out with his teeth, Alice gently nudged him until he rolled onto his side, coughing up a lung.

"You had to do it," Daniel complained, reaching for his water pouch and chugging as much as he could.

He sat up, trying to get his bearings. Even by the glow of the single remaining wall light, the situation became obvious: the tunnel was completely blocked.

"Great going . . . Just great."

Alice sneezed.

"Bless you." He craned his neck, looking up to see how far the roof now extended. Quite a way by the look of things, which was good. "At least we won't be running out of air anytime soon," he said.

He got to his feet, scratching around for some miraculous alternate route out of there. There was none, but at least–

What the heck was that?

In the dim light, a burnished artifact, silvery and ghost-like, sat embedded in the newly exposed rock face.

Daniel edged closer. He had no memory of the hundreds of artifacts he'd no doubt dredged up from the mines before the wipe, but he'd bet a thousand Passava roots he'd never seen anything like this.

Carefully scraping away the dirt with his bare fingers, he exposed the curved metal edges of a mechanical fossil. He could feel it vibrating, as though it were alive; as though it wanted to leap out of the rock at him–

The Overseers would want to see this.

"Of course!" Daniel exclaimed, fumbling around in his tool belt. The Overseers would gladly dig them out for this!

He pulled out a familiar-looking device, a small, notched cylinder that Blink had first shown him over a week ago, or however long it had been when he'd first taken Alice down into the Snake. What the heck had he called it?

A Regulator.

A tracking device to alert the Overseers to your impending death. Problem was, they already knew where he was, but they didn't know what he'd found. There had to be a commlink on this thing somewhere–there!

He set it to transmit and, as loud as he could, cried, "Relic!"

9
THE SILVER RELIC

It took what felt like forever to dig him and Alice out.

The Overseer raked a battered finger over the crumbling sediment of the mine wall, exposing the ancient artifact to the damp air. The object appeared to be a silver hexagon, about the size of Daniel's hand, with a crystalline, almost snowflake-like pattern folded into the metal. Although knowing what it looked like did nothing to explain what it actually was.

The Overseer cocked its head, setting off a brief but shrill click before making a series of deep, animalistic noises. This time there was no translation. If it was speech, none of the grubs had ever learned to speak it, but it certainly elicited a response from other members of the Overseer troop. An exchange of grunts over the commlink sounded more like an argument, until finally the Overseer stretched out an armored hand and tried prying the artifact from the rock.

The silver relic would not budge.

Undeterred, the Overseer pulled out his blast-pike, rammed it into the mine wall, and fired.

Craaaackkkk!

Daniel threw an arm over his face as the surface layer of rock shattered into a thousand pieces.

While the dust settled, the Overseer tried again. Still the artifact would not move.

For his part, Alice was both unimpressed and growing increasingly bored. The Hammertail let out a long, self-satisfied fart.

The Overseer slowly glanced over his shoulder, before turning his icy attention back to Daniel. He aimed his blast-pike at the artifact.

Daniel knew what he had to do. "Fetch another drote!" he called to the grubs gathered at the entrance.

The Overseer walked back to his troop, ready to meet the cohort of Overseers who were marching down the Snake to see the discovery for themselves.

Whatever it was he'd found–it was important.

Daniel worked quickly. Unclipping a new scent marker from his tool belt, he dabbed it in two or three places around the silver relic, just as before. Only, the blast from the Overseer's weapon had injected so much heat into the rock face, the gloop was already starting to smoke–

Daniel blew on it, waved his hands–whatever he could

think of to try to clear the smoke away. The last thing he needed was a repeat of the Alice fiasco all over again–

Daniel froze, the silver relic gleaming in his eyes.

It had moved! It was still moving, vibrating rapidly, dust falling from it like sand in an hourglass.

Maybe he could get it out? Without thinking, Daniel stretched out his hand, only to feel a wave of power surge through his fingers.

"Ouch!"

He jerked his hand back. What was this thing?

With an almighty *whompff* the silver relic blasted out of the rock face, smashing into Daniel's chest, knocking him flying–

He hit the ground with a crunch, and lay stunned, wheezing for air.

Maybe somewhere else in the universe, that might have been enough to prompt a little help, but here in the relic mine the rules were different. The Overseers ignored him, oblivious to what had just happened and concerned more with the quality of a drote one of the grubs had returned with and whether any of the other grubs could locate the bait-box–

Daniel pulled himself up onto one knee, searching in the dirt. The silver relic–where was it? If he could just–

Craaaackkkk!

Daniel glanced back over his shoulder. The mine wall crumbled, sloughing off in sheets like skin peeling off a snake, revealing a massive doorway sinking down into the earth and a hidden chamber cloaked in shadow beyond its threshold.

10
BEYOND THE THRESHOLD

The entire troop of Overseers lit up their blast-pikes in a defensive crackle of electricity–but nothing emerged from the chamber except for a cool, damp breeze. As grubs from all over the Workings moved closer to see the discovery for themselves, one of the Overseers declared, “Sixteen thirty-three, go check it out.”

With absurd pride in his voice, Pinch Servilles said, “Yes, sir,” and, grabbing the F-light from his belt, launched an orb and headed into the chamber.

Alice let out a vicious growl as he passed by.

“You tell him, Alice,” Blink remarked from the shadow of the Overseers.

Daniel held out his hand, eager for help getting up, but Pinch just ignored him on his way past. “You’d better find that relic, Coldstar, or you’ll pay for it.”

"What a dootbag," Blink whispered under his breath.

"Careful, Darkada," Pinch taunted, standing at the threshold to the darkness. "Wouldn't want you to take another beating."

Pinch peered into the darkness, but the chamber was so vast that the F-light's feeble beam couldn't penetrate very far. There were shapes. Rows and rows of them, but it was impossible to know what they were exactly at this distance.

Daniel gingerly tried pulling himself up. He didn't just hurt, he had stars in his eyes, and when he tried to stand his ribs bristled with pain. He grunted, clutching his chest to find–

Cold, hard metal pulsing under his fingers.

Daniel glanced down. The silver relic had secured itself to his dugs. "What the . . ."

Inconspicuously, he tried prying it off, but it just made the pain worse. He tried again, harder this time. Nothing.

A finger of ice ran down his spine. If he couldn't get this thing off, would the Overseers disappear him again–or just kill him for it?

"Master Overseer, sir!" Pinch called out. "Request a LightEye, sir!"

The Overseers argued among themselves, angry grunts flying back and forth over their commlink.

"Forty-one eighty-two, report," demanded one of them.

Daniel couldn't look at them. He crawled around, with his hands in the dirt, and hoped they wouldn't notice there was a bigger problem. "I'm still trying to locate the relic," he said, short of breath.

"Forty-one eighty-two, help sixteen thirty-three."

Oh no . . .

"Forty-one eighty-two, respond."

Did they know something was up? Reluctantly, Daniel stopped what he was doing and got to his feet without saying a word. Keeping his back to them, he fired up his own F-light and staggered toward the entrance.

How in the universe was he going to keep Pinch Servilles from seeing what was pinned to his chest?

The truth of the matter was that he wasn't. Pinch saw it immediately, glinting under the shine of Daniel's F-light. And that look in his eye; a peculiar kind of joy that came from knowing Daniel was in trouble.

"Sorry about Alice," Pinch said sarcastically. "I had no idea he'd bolt for you like that–what are you doing with that relic?"

"Can you help me?" Daniel asked, trying not to sound like he was begging. "Please."

"Why would I do that?" Pinch replied, taking a step closer, his eyes alive with excitement.

There was that anger again, boiling inside Daniel, eager to knock a few teeth down this kid's throat. "Okay, tell them," said Daniel, "if you want to find out how fast the guards can get over here and save you." He couldn't help it. It just came out.

It was all Pinch needed, just knowing that Daniel was afraid. "They trust me," he explained, his voice filled with peculiar confidence. "Follow my lead from now on and perhaps I can help you. We'd make a powerful team, you and I."

This kid was so deluded he actually thought he had some kind of bargaining power with the Overseers? Unbelievable.

"Sixteen thirty-three, report!"

Pinch smiled. "Time to make a choice, Coldstar," he said.

Daniel took a moment to think about it, but there really was no other way of saying it. "You're an idiot," he said.

Pinch stepped back as though he were the one in control, pointed at Daniel, and screamed. "He's stealing the relic!"

The Overseers aimed their blast-pikes squarely at Daniel. Marching at him in a line, there was nowhere to go, nowhere to hide.

"It was an accident!" Daniel protested, facing them. "I didn't know it was going to happen!"

"Forty-one eighty-two, hand over the relic!"

They were just paces away now, the entire troop, electricity crackling from weapon to weapon.

"I can't!" Daniel explained, hot tears spilling from his eyes. "It's stuck." He tore at the silver relic but it would not budge.

"Forty-one eighty-two, comply!"

"It won't move," he said, falling to his knees, defeated.

The Overseers loomed over him, so close; the stomach-churning reek of dead meat filled his nostrils.

Daniel watched their rusted fingers tense on the triggers, and instinctively threw his arms up, crossing them over his face as though such a feeble gesture could protect him.

"Here, take it!" he cried, bracing himself for more pain than he'd ever known.

And that was when a miracle happened.

A sheet of spinning air formed right in front of him; a shield of pure fury, howling like a living creature, and just like a tornado, it swept up everything in its path. Bits of shattered stone and rent metal whirled around its circumference, reaching such colossal speed that the debris glowed white hot, casting off lightning bolts and slicing through solid rock.

Pinch and Blink instinctively dropped to the ground, clawing their fingers into the dirt in hopes of protecting themselves. The force of it all chopped through the Overseers' weapons, leaving them defenseless. One by one, their feet left the ground. Struggling against the whirlwind's wrath, they tried to flee.

Whompff!

Daniel's head snapped back with a jolt as a shock wave blasted out from his body, exploding like a rocket motor, hurling the Overseers through the air and crushing them against the mine walls.

And when they stopped struggling, and there was no life left inside their rotting armor, the shield of air disappeared in a puff, the bodies of the Overseers slumped to the ground–and all the awesome power that had protected him rested once again inside the silver relic attached firmly to Daniel Coldstar's chest.

11

POINT OF NO RETURN

Daniel had never seen so many mouths hanging open all at once.

The stunned silence surrounding him was so overwhelming, only the distant thrum of grubs hammering away in other parts of the mine told Daniel that he hadn't suddenly gone deaf.

Daniel couldn't figure out if they were afraid of him or in awe. He glanced over at Pinch; he looked like he'd been snatched by a Nightwatcher, blood drained from his face. He stumbled back against the mine wall and tore off back the way they'd all come.

"Hey, should we–er, stop him?" said Blink.

"What's the point?" said Henegan, stepping over one of the Overseer bodies. "When this bunch don't report in, I think the others are going to figure it out."

Nails glanced from one body to the next. "We're so dead. . . ."

Fix ran up to Daniel, getting right in his face, waving his arms around excitedly, and raving in gibberish.

"I don't speak Jarabic," Daniel snapped, frustrated. "You know that."

"He says, do it again," said Blink.

"Do what again?"

"Whatever you just did."

"I didn't do anything!"

"Yeah, sure you didn't." Henegan picked at his teeth. "They're all just taking a nap."

Fix grabbed Daniel's arms and tried forcing him. Daniel shook him off. "Cut it out."

"Just do the thing with the arms," Blink explained, clearing Fix out of the way.

"What thing?"

Blink tried his best not to get angry. "Did you just kill a bunch of Overseers or not?" He gestured to Fix. "Show him."

Fix clumsily crossed his arms over the top of his head. "Do it," he urged. "Do it."

Daniel sighed. "All right," he said.

"Stand back, ladies," said Henegan, pinning himself flat against the tunnel wall. "This could get interesting."

Daniel waited for them to get clear before doing what they wanted.

Sheepishly, he raised his arms up, crossed them—but nothing happened. "Satisfied?"

Minds were racing. There had to be a way to activate the relic. "He was kneeling when it happened," said Nails. "Try kneeling."

Daniel had had enough. "I'm not kneeling! Don't you get it? I don't control this thing. If anything, it's controlling me. I can't even take if off!" He yanked at the silver relic again and again, but it was stuck fast.

"Dee, you have to figure it out," said Blink, a wobble in his voice, "or Nails is right: we're all dead."

"What if we go this way . . . ?" Henegan stood in the doorway, peering into the dark chamber. "Maybe there's a way out."

"Or not," said Nails, but that didn't stop a handful or so of grubs from gathering around, weighing the option of taking a chance.

"We have no idea where that leads," Blink warned.

Daniel shrugged. "Neither do they. And if we go back to the Racks, we're all dead anyway." He crossed into the black, his F-light failing to penetrate much beyond a few paces around him. "I'm the one they want," he said. "Blame it all on me. Maybe I can stay hidden long enough to figure out how to work this thing, and come back for you."

Blink marched after him. "You don't get to decide that, we all do."

"Then decide," Daniel replied, "but I'm going. I don't

have a choice." At his side, Alice's hot breath blasted over his hand. How a trabasaur of that size had crept up on him was a mystery.

Nails stood with him, pale faced and unable to mask the quiver in his voice; he knew what he was getting into, but somehow he found the courage anyway. "Don't worry about tomorrow, eh? We might not see it anyway."

"That's the spirit," Henegan said, firing up his own F-light. "Besides, if they don't disappear us, they'll wipe us so fast we won't even remember we found this place. Any takers on how far we get? I'm in for a stick."

Blink shook his head. "Shut up."

There were seven in all in the end, including Alice, with Fix and Gungy Wamp making up the last two. Choky stayed back behind the doorway; he didn't have the guts. "See you back at the Racks," he kept saying, in between wheezy laughs, while all around him grubs were doing the serious work of placing bets with Ogle Kog on how far the group would make it.

Everything felt different in here. The floor was polished smooth, the seams between the sections barely noticeable at first. Each footstep made a kind of clanging sound that echoed in a hollow somewhere beneath the surface. They were walking on metal; like the deck of some enormous vessel. As their eyes adjusted to the dark, they spied ginormous metal ribs projecting up into the unknowable blackness above.

As they moved deeper into the space, through armored corridors and smaller chambers, it became apparent that nobody had been keeping track of where they were going. Heading back now would be close to impossible–not that anybody had been planning on it.

Until they rounded the next corner, and came face-to-face with a waiting Overseer.

12
ARMY OF DARKNESS

"Look out!" Blink cried, bundling Daniel out of the way.

The two boys hit the ground. But the Overseer they had just spotted didn't so much as twitch. Alice whipped around, knocking the Overseer's helmet clean off.

A plume of dust followed it, arcing through the air before landing with a clatter right in front of Daniel's face.

While the other boys scattered, the F-lights trying to keep up with them like a swarm of panicked fireflies, Daniel glanced up to see–hundreds? Thousands? Everywhere he looked stood row upon row of Overseers, all covered in a thick blanket of dust–

None of them were moving.

"Alice!" Daniel cried, scrambling to his feet. "Hey! Will you quit it?"

"They're just suits of armor!" He grabbed the leash and yanked on it. "See?"

He struck one of the Overseers. The figure crashed to the ground, armor plating tumbling in all directions, spilling dust across the ground.

Reluctantly, Alice quit stomping his victim to bits, but not before getting in one last kick.

"Feel better?"

Alice flicked an ear.

Blink couldn't believe what he was seeing. "This is what they've been looking for?"

"There must be an entire army down here," Nails said, gladly taking Henegan's helping hand up.

"How long do you think they've been here?"

Gungy the Mute, peering closely at the dents and scratches pitting the armor, said, "Since the dawn of time."

With the exception of Daniel, who didn't know any better, the other grubs all gave Gungy their undivided attention.

"Wait a minute," said Blink. "You can speak?"

"Of course."

"And you never said anything?"

"You're Gungy Wamp–the Mute," said Henegan, butting in. "That means you don't speak."

Gungy shrugged. "I like being left alone."

Somewhere in the darkness something clattered to the ground, its echo taking so long to return that the chamber had to be truly vast.

The boys froze, waiting for what might follow.

"None of us are going to be alone for much longer," said Daniel in a whisper, "if we don't get going."

No one argued. They set off so quickly they were almost running. With every step, more and more figures loomed out of the darkness. Overseers in shapes and sizes they'd never seen before–some with four arms, others with no arms at all–lines and lines of them, all standing to attention as though on a parade ground.

"This is creepy. . . ." Nails said, under his breath. "There're so many of them."

The hair on the back of Daniel's neck stood on end, but he wasn't about to give in to it. Alice, on the other hand–

The sixteen-ton Hammertail suddenly switched gears and shot off in a different direction altogether.

"What the–Hey!"

Blink grabbed Daniel by the arm. "Let him go."

"He'll get lost."

"We're already lost! If he wants out, he'll catch up," said Blink. "Who cares?"

"Maybe he smells something."

"It's Alice," Blink replied. "Of course he smells something–"

Click . . . click . . . click.

Daniel's heart sank. "Oh, what's he done now?"

Click . . . click . . . click.

"Alice!" Daniel cried.

But Henegan waved his fingers over his neck, urging him to can it. "I don't think that's Alice," he whispered.

Click . . . click . . . click.

"They found us," said Gungy. "Run!"

But no sooner had he taken a few steps than a whoosh of air blasted over their heads.

"WHO DISTURBS?" the Nightwatcher crowed, its voice vibrating in every grub's bones. "Who disturbs?"

Swooping in with its talons glinting in the F-lights, the Nightwatcher sank its claws into Gungy Wamp's shoulders and yanked him off his feet.

With a beat of its wings, the boy was already six paces off the ground.

And within a second he was gone completely, leaving nothing behind but the sound of his screaming.

ATTACK OF THE NIGHTWATCHERS

The beat of massive wings thumped in the dark. More were coming.

Daniel ducked behind another set of dusty Overseer armor, reaching for his F-light launcher.

Setting it to retrieval mode, he aimed it at the light, pulled the trigger, and–

>MALFUNCTION<

"No, no, no . . ."

He fiddled with the device, but nothing worked. His F-light refused to return to its launcher, instead shining down on his hiding spot even brighter than before–

Whoosh!

The armor rattled as a Nightwatcher swooped over Daniel's head, talons just inches from his skin.

Forget it. He tossed the launcher aside and ran, zigzagging

in and out of the lines of Overseers, acutely aware that another Nightwatcher was breathing down his neck–

More screaming.

Fix and Nails were being lifted off their feet by a single Nightwatcher, one grub in each claw, but Blink hurled an Overseer helmet right at its snout.

The Nightwatcher dropped the grubs, caught the helmet, and slung it right back, smashing Blink in the side of the head.

He staggered, unable to figure out how to even stand up straight, incapable of fending off the next attack.

Daniel didn't stop to think. Yanking a hefty breastplate out of the collapsing shell of another long-dead Overseer, he plowed headlong into Blink, pulling him under it just as–

Wham!

A fist-sized dent punched through the armor, so deep it barely missed Daniel's face.

Wham! Wham!

His arms buckled with each frenzied blow. He pulled his legs up under the plate and pushed with his feet–

Wham!

"Blink!" Daniel shrieked. "I can't hold this much longer!"

Wham! Wham!

"Blink!"

Blink, barely able to focus, reached out to help when a second set of metal claws tried lunging underneath to snatch him away.

Ka-choom. Ka-choom. Ka-choom.

That wasn't a Nightwatcher. Something else was going on. The ground shook beneath them; light began pouring into the massive chamber.

Ka-choom. Ka-choom. Ka-choom.

Armor rattled.

And all the while, Alice played with the pressure plates in the floor, enjoying the way he was able to make things happen like turn the lights on and off every time he stomped on one.

But all that changed the moment the platforms rose up out of the ground. Humongous armored suits stood on each one, more like vehicles than body armor. They made Alice look like a drote in comparison, but it would take more than that to intimidate a Hammertail.

Alice quickly smashed the closest one to smithereens before the platform could even deliver it all the way to the top.

With gigantic plates of armor crashing in every direction, the startled Nightwatchers took to the air before they became targets themselves.

Now was their chance! Blink and Daniel tossed their makeshift shield aside and helped each other up–but which way to go? There were halls and metal steps, all dotted around the perimeter. But which one to take?

He glanced around, about to pick a direction at random, when he noticed an exit opening up into the familiar jagged rock of a cave and connecting tunnels. "There," he said.

Together they made a run for it.

Inside the tunnel, the ground was uneven, loose in places and shaking violently, but neither boy let it slow them down.

Blink glanced back over his shoulder. "Come on!" he yelled.

Nails and Fix hobbled after them, blood glistening from the rips in their dugs. There was no sign of Henegan, maybe he was already out–

Daniel darted in and out of the armor, keeping one eye on the Nightwatchers circling overhead. There was open space between him and the staircase out of here. He'd have to be quick if he was going to make it.

"Don't stop!" Daniel warned, tearing out into the open. "Just keep going!"

It was the last thing he said before the ground opened up and swallowed him.

14
UPSIDE DOWN

Daniel tumbled through the gaping earth, his mouth filling with dirt. He clawed at the smothering rubble, desperate to breathe until–

Whoosh!

An ice-cold blast of air opened up his airway. He was in free fall, hurtling into a void filled with the sound of stone hammering into the ground and shattering into a thousand pieces.

He was sure the same thing would happen to him any second now and there was nothing he could do about it.

He flailed around, tears streaking from his eyes, the memory of Fix clumsily yelling in his ear, "Do it!"

The silver relic had protected him once before; maybe it would do it again.

Daniel closed his eyes, clutching the artifact on his chest, and silently begged–*please work, please work!*

Any second, and this was going to hurt; this was going to hurt really badly–

He crossed his arms in front of him and, with every nerve in his body on fire, Daniel raged. "Arghhhh!"

Whompff!

Howling louder than Daniel ever could, unleashing a power that struck more terror into his heart than his oncoming extinction, the air spun beneath him at cyclonic speed–

Wham!

Daniel found himself launched into the storm created by the relic just at the moment of impact. He was cushioned by its fury, coming nose to nose with the ground before rebounding into the air, and landed more or less on his feet.

But it wasn't over yet–everything that had fallen through the hole after him started smashing into the ground from every side.

He glanced up. A boulder the size of a GoLoader was coming right at him. With nowhere to hide, and no time to run, Daniel's instinct kicked in. Sweeping one arm over his head, he wielded the cyclone like a shield, batting the boulder away at colossal speed. It smashed into the other side of the chamber, before rolling to a stop.

Daniel took a moment to catch his breath while his accomplishment sank in. He laughed like he'd never laughed in his life. At least, what he could remember of his life.

His actions alone didn't control the silver relic; his feelings and his thoughts were just as important–as though this thing could read his mind.

Daniel had to *want* to protect himself.

Now he understood! He couldn't help it; he punched the air. "Yeah!" Ouch. Maybe that was a little too much. His ribs couldn't take the joy.

Heck, everything hurt more than usual and–where the drote was he? And where were his friends?

The terrain didn't make any sense. He stood in a honeycomb of collapsed passages, too many to count, while the enormous boulder he'd swatted away appeared to have rolled . . . uphill.

He shut the relic off by thinking of something else, letting the cyclone blow itself out.

"Blink?" No reply.

His voice echoed down the passageways, bouncing from one tunnel to the next until it sounded as though a multitude of Daniel Coldstars were calling Blink's name.

"Anyone? Hello!"

"Anyone? Hello!"

"Anyone? Hello!"

"Anyone? Hello!"

"Anyone? Hello!"

Now he was just creeping himself out. Okay, so he was alone. Blink had to be down here somewhere, but where?

There were a handful of passages within a few paces of where he was standing. It was a wonder he hadn't fallen straight down into one. One passage climbed sharply, another dipped away. Which one was the best was anyone's guess. Except–

Over there . . . the faint, warm glow of–what?

Was that Blink? Why didn't he answer Daniel's call? Maybe he was hurt. Daniel took a step toward the glow before forcing himself to stop.

Wait a minute. Had the Nightwatchers found him? He waited and watched.

No, the light didn't move. It held steady.

Was that . . . daylight? Had he found the way out?

In a time before this one, before the darkness, he vaguely remembered a brilliant, shining light hanging in a vast open space he seemed to recall had been "the sky." It'd been so many years since he'd seen it; so long ago that he wondered if it was just his imagination playing tricks. But then he remembered that warmth, that prickling sensation across his skin, and he figured it had to be remembering something real.

Of all the memories, the Overseers hadn't wiped that one.

Could it be bright enough to be daylight? He wouldn't know unless he looked.

The passage was narrower than any mining tunnel, and the solid rock walls were smoother too. The surface felt glassy, as though some incredible force had melted it and it had then rehardened.

But with every step things only grew stranger.

The farther he went, the more that gravity seemed to be changing direction. By the time he was halfway down the passage, he was walking on the wall.

The problem was that when he peered around the corner, it wasn't daylight that he found–but artificial light spilling from a cannon-like object that looked like it was about to open fire.

Daniel pulled his head back before he got shot in the face, but no blast came.

"Wait a minute. . . ." That thing looked familiar. He poked his head carefully back around the corner. "A gravity generator?"

He'd never seen one in the mines. They were used on ships and asteroids to create a field when the gravity was too low. Was he on an asteroid? Asteroids were nothing like planets. Going outside would mean trying to find some protection and a little air to breathe. Otherwise there would be no escape and–

Wait. How did he know any of this?

Had they forgotten to wipe another memory? No, that wasn't it. Everything changed the moment . . . the silver relic–

What was that?

Behind him, coming from the opposite passage, there

was a low, electrical hum drifting hypnotically down a shaft even narrower than the last.

It had a steep incline, but there didn't appear to be too far to climb.

Maybe he could just peer over the top and see what was going on? If he didn't have any luck here, he could always find his way back to the honeycomb. There were a thousand other routes to try.

Daniel threw himself forward to begin the climb and immediately regretted it. Gravity inside this passage pulled him in another direction entirely–

He careened out of control–shooting upward, headfirst into who knows where, all sense of knowing up from down completely gone.

Tumbling back out into the open, he landed in a heap on a metal deck.

Dazed, Daniel tried to make sense of where he was, but all he really knew for sure was that he had landed in front of a human face suspended inside a large glass tube. Rotating slowly, it seemed conscious of the world around it, and as it turned toward Daniel it locked its eyes upon him, mouthing silently: *Help me! Help me!*

The face was Blink's.

15
FACE-TO-FACE

Daniel scrambled back as fast as he could until there was nowhere else to go in the passage.

How had they caught Blink so fast? What had they done to him–? His face . . . trapped inside a glass jar, no bigger than the ones they used to pickle Ridgeback eggs, hung from a wire like an eerie decoration. How was that even possible?

But Blink's was not the only face confined to a glass prison–Daniel was surrounded. Henegan's face spun around in another jar, and Nails's face occupied the one next to that. And then there were the disappeared; grubs he suddenly remembered he hadn't seen in forever.

They were all here, every single one; thousands of grubs all fighting to get a better a look at Daniel, all begging him for help, each one part of the intricate workings of a gigantic machine that defied a simple explanation. The jars were suspended on long, thin telescopic arms, while a spider's web of cables and hoses crisscrossed in between them. Every now and then tiny mechanical bugs would emerge from the wiring, examine a jar, make some kind of adjustment, and scurry off. The entire apparatus sat under a vast metal umbrella with platforms and staircases bolted to its surface for whoever tended to this monstrosity.

With his back pressed against cold stone, Daniel struggled to his feet.

He stood bolted to the ground for what seemed like an eternity, trying to make sense of it, but nothing about this place made sense, especially when he noticed a single face hidden in the crowd. . . .

It was his own.

Daniel watched himself and reached out–wrapping his fingers tightly around the glass flask, prying the object free.

His own face gazed up at him from the palm of his hand. What was this thing? A hologram? It didn't appear to have a generator. It was sealed at both ends.

"Wait a minute. . . ."

He shook it like a snow globe. The face disappeared in a cloud of sparkling particles before condensing back down into a face.

"Holocules," he whispered. Literally holographic molecules; microscopic particles of programmed energy and matter that floated freely in the air like dust, waiting for the order to form up.

He felt a breath so close to his ear that every hair, across every inch of his body, stood on end. Daniel spun around.

No one there.

"Daniel . . ." a voice with the timbre of grinding metal whispered in his other ear.

Daniel spun to face the other direction–

Still no one there.

"Who are you?" Daniel called out.

The voice sounded cruel and amused when it whispered back, "The better question is: who are you?"

"I'm Daniel Coldstar–"

"That is a name," the voice admonished, "but it is not who you are."

Every time the voice spoke, it did so in each ear, sometimes switching mid-sentence, and each time so close that he could feel a presence over his shoulder, little hairs buzzing on the inside of his ear.

Yet still that presence remained invisible.

"I don't understand," said Daniel.

"Where are you from?" the sinister voice asked.

"I don't know," Daniel replied, surprised by the level of his own anger. "They won't let me remember!"

"Who are they?"

"The Overseers," Daniel responded.

"Perhaps it is not they who hide your memories. . . . Perhaps it is you."

That didn't make sense. "Why would I do that?"

The voice whispered back, "Why would you want to remember a family that betrayed you, that cast you aside like worthless garbage?"

The words struck Daniel harder than any physical blow. He searched his heart, but the answers weren't there. And all these questions sent him into a panic, which he fought very hard to overcome.

He gazed upon the glass vial containing his holocule, and, seeing it through his tears, he said, "What is this?"

The voice slithered from ear to ear. "That. Is. Your. Mind."

"And if I break it?"

"You die."

Daniel glanced around, wiping the tears on his sleeve. "I don't believe you," he said.

A cruel, whispering laugh echoed in his ears. "You are our property," it said. "Your body is a machine; your mind stays here. Leave, and your body will die, but it can be replaced. There is no escape."

"You're lying," said Daniel, tucking the glass flask into his utility belt just in case. He craned his neck to get a good look at the far recesses of the machine's superstructure. "Why won't you show your face?"

"What purpose would that serve?"

“Because,” said Daniel, reassuringly touching the relic on his chest, “you know you can’t stop me while I have this. And I’d like to see your face when you try to lie to me again.”

“Why would I lie?”

“I don’t know,” said Daniel, searching. There had to be another way out of here somehow.

“An Aegis is a feeble weapon,” the voice whispered. “It is no match for me.”

There–a staircase leading up to all platforms with a bridge suspended out to the side and disappearing into the cavern wall. Daniel broke into a run, the voice staying with him, taunting him. “There is nothing up there for you but pain and sorrow.”

No different from being down here then, Daniel concluded, but he wasn’t about to voice his thoughts. Something deep down inside told him to stop communicating with–whatever this was. Everything he said came back twisted, trying to confuse him.

Resolutely, darting up the stairs, his heart racing–three flights, two, a few more steps–he rounded the corner, saw the bridge, and–

Standing on the other side of it, an imposing figure, cloaked in darkness, calmly waiting for him.

Daniel pulled up short. An Overseer?

No. A small glimmer of light revealed a twisted version of Daniel’s own relic pinned to its chest and, for one brief moment–a face made entirely of jagged edges.

No, not an Overseer. This was something else.

Still with that voice like grinding metal, and still right in his ear, the figure whispered, "I am impressed you have made it this far. I advised that you be terminated. Your reeducation was a failure. You never should have been placed back into the general population. You have jeopardized everything."

Daniel refused to respond. He knew more Overseers were coming. This was just a tactic to try to slow him down. It wouldn't work. Daniel was too busy trying to figure out how to get past him.

The figure hissed. "Vega Seftis sees promise. You may still serve the Sinja in new ways."

The Sinja? "Who? Are they like Overseers?"

"We are the Sinja," the figure spat. "And they serve us!"

Daniel couldn't figure out if he was amused or angry, until the twisted relic mounted on the Sinja's chest shrieked as though it were alive.

Pulling dust, debris, and anything else that was lying around into a swirling maelstrom, the Sinja grew a legion of phantom limbs.

Daniel had never seen anything like it. His eyes widened, his hands shook. Unsure of himself, he grew unsteady on his feet, but he wasn't about to turn back now.

Bringing his forearm up in front of his face, Daniel set the air swirling to create the most powerful vortex shield he could muster.

The dark figure came at him at inhuman speed, its phantom limbs balling their fists, leaving trails of dust in their wake.

Daniel tasted the lining of his stomach in his mouth. He didn't have a clue how he was going to defend himself, but he had to even the odds somehow.

If he could wield air like a shield, could he launch it like a weapon?

There was only one way to find out. Daniel pulled his arm back before slinging a tornado at the figure with such force that he dropped to his own knees.

The spinning blade of air hurtled across the bridge, meeting the dark figure in a shock wave of such incredible power that it sliced the Sinja in two. Limbs tumbled in all directions and then–*poof*, the storm collapsed, leaving nothing but a faint breeze in its wake.

There was no figure. Like the holocule faces trapped inside the glass vials below, the Sinja had been an illusion as well.

Daniel stood up, the anger and fear that had been feeding on him lifted from his shoulders. He felt confident and strong in ways that did not fully make sense. But in this moment, listening to and trusting his inner voice, he had been changed.

With a tremor still tugging at his legs, he walked carefully across the bridge, aware of every sound, every rock fall–every misplaced chink of light. By the time he reached the other side, he was fully aware of something blundering around in the dark, just around the next corner.

This time he waited, only just managing to stop himself from attacking when he realized who it was.

"Blink?"

"Dee, where have you been? I've been looking all over for you!"

"Things got a little complicated–"

Blink caught a glimpse over Daniel's shoulder of the massive machine he'd left behind. "What's that thing?"

"It's nothing." He grabbed Blink by the arm, shoving him in the other direction. "We have to get out of here."

"No kidding," said Blink. "I think I found the exit."

16

OUT OF REACH

Daniel closed his eyes and drank it in. "Fresh air," he said. "Right?"

The opening sat far above their heads. A pale light flickered from somewhere farther up inside the shaft. It certainly wasn't daylight, but as Blink said, maybe it was nighttime outside.

The problem was how to reach it. There was no way of climbing to it directly. The rock face underneath the opening curved inward. Unless they could figure out how to defy gravity and climb upside down by the time they reached the top, they would never make it.

"Maybe we should go back the way we came," Blink suggested.

"Why don't we just turn ourselves in to the Overseers,

save them the hassle of having to find us?" said Daniel.

"They don't have a clue where we are," Blink snapped. "There's more than enough time."

"They know," Daniel insisted, trying his hardest to keep his anger in check. "Trust me." Surveying the chamber, he said, "We're going to have to jump." He pointed to a ledge on the wall opposite the opening. "From there," he said.

It was easier to reach. The climb went straight up. But there had to be a good twenty paces between the ledge and the source of the light. They'd never be able to jump that distance. "Are you crazy?" Blink protested.

"You got a better idea?"

"Yes. We go back and we find something to use as a ladder."

Daniel ignored Blink and started climbing. "Have fun back at the Racks," he said.

"You are one stubborn drote," Blink replied under his breath.

Daniel just kept climbing, Blink eventually following him all the way up to the top. Before he had time to get cold feet, Daniel took the utility hook on his belt and latched it onto Blink.

"We take a running jump," Daniel said quickly. "Ready?"

"Wait a minute, what the heck do you have in mind?"

Daniel quit listening. "Jump or I push."

"Do you even know if this is going to work?"

"Of course I don't know, I've never done this before!"

Blink peered over the edge. "That's a heck of a fall," Daniel said. "One–"

"Okay, okay!" Blink took three paces back. "Two–"

Screaming in absolute terror, Blink and Daniel ran forward, launching themselves at the opening on the other side.

Whompff!

A shock wave blasted out from the relic on Daniel's chest, lifting them up and hurling them into the airshaft, arms and legs flailing.

Landing in a crumpled heap, barely able to move, they each rolled onto their backs, trying to breathe.

Daniel pulled his bloodied face out of the dirt. "You okay?" he asked gingerly.

Blink rolled his eyes back into his head. "You suck," he croaked.

Everything hurt–every single inch. Unclipping himself from Blink's belt, Daniel struggled to sit up.

A steady stream of cool air whistled past his ears.

Daniel glanced around.

There, an exit at the end of the tunnel, exposing a vast velvety blanket of deep blues and streaks of pink sprinkled with endless twinkling lights.

His breath caught in his throat. He recognized them! "Are . . . those . . . stars?"

Blink rolled over to see what he was talking about. His mouth hung open. "I don't believe it," he said. "We're out."

SUNSRISE OVER A BROKEN WORLD

The two boys stepped out onto the surface of a world that was hard to call a planet, although, once upon a time, it must have been one.

Beneath the infinite haze stretching from horizon to horizon that must've been the sky, the shattered remains of what was once a planet curved upward in both directions. The planet, which long ago had probably been a ball shape like any other planet, had been whittled down until all that was left was a vast crescent; a planet-sized orange peel floating in space, while all around the further remains of its shattered body had formed a thousand moons and flocks of asteroids, skipping and tumbling around one another, drawn together by the forces of their own gravity.

On the horizon, the lights of a distant outpost illuminated the bellies of a swarm of tiny craft, zipping to and fro from the massive hulk of a freighter.

Blink went to step outside, but Daniel stopped him. "Wait."

"What's wrong?"

Daniel rested a hand on his utility belt, and the pouch containing his holocule. The warning had been clear: if he stepped outside, he was dead. The same went for any of the grubs. Daniel didn't think much about putting his own life in danger, but his friends? That was something else.

Whether or not that threat had been true, there was really only one way to test it.

"Wait here, okay?" he said.

"For what?"

"Just do it."

"Who made you boss?" Blink snapped.

"Uh, this thing?" said Daniel, gesturing to the powerful relic pinned to his chest. "Give me two minutes."

Blink threw up his hands.

"After that, do what you want. Just. Stay. There."

"Fine. Two minutes."

Daniel held his breath when he stepped outside, the air so cold that his eyes started watering. He reached into his belt for his mining goggles. They steamed up as soon as he put them on, which was probably a good thing because there were so many planetary fragments tumbling past in the sky that it was downright dizzying, and now he couldn't see them.

Expecting the worst, he stepped gingerly out onto the surface of the ruined planet. As more time went by, he took more and more hesitant steps, until he'd gone a good ways, maybe twenty or thirty paces, and he stopped.

He waited. And he waited. And before long, nothing happened. He knew it! The threat of death had been a lie.

Keeping his back to Blink, he pulled the glowing holocule from its pouch, watching his own face spinning around inside the glass tube.

He tossed it on the ground and stamped on it as hard as he could. The glass shattered, releasing the brightly sparkling pinpricks of light. They swirled around, trying to form an image, before a gust of wind caught them and blew them away.

Daniel stood watching the stars when Blink came up quietly beside him.

"Didn't I tell you to stay over there?"

"Since when did I ever listen to you? We can't stay here much longer, you know."

Daniel nodded.

The ground sloped away not far from the tunnel entrance, a mix of scree and ice that proved difficult to walk on, but neither of them cared. They walked in silence, just a couple of battle-scarred soldiers soaking in their surroundings. So much open space; so much freedom. It was so different from the Racks and the mines.

Eventually Blink couldn't stay silent any longer. "You want to tell me what that was all about back there?" he asked.

"Not really, no."

"You want to tell me where we're going?"

"No clue."

"Can I make a suggestion?"

Daniel shrugged. "Sure," he said.

"That ship over there has to head somewhere, right?" he said. "Might be good to be on it when it does."

Daniel stopped in his tracks, jabbing an accusing finger at the uncountable stars. "And go where, Blink? Where? Which one's home?"

"I don't know. I hadn't really thought that far!" Blink spat. "But anywhere's better than where we just came from."

"Let's hope so." Daniel rubbed a trembling hand over his exhausted face. Finding a place to sit, he reached into his utility belt for some water. Instead he found a hole in the pouch.

Blink checked his own supply–empty.

Neither of them said it, but they both knew that if they didn't find water or food soon, they weren't going to make it to any ship.

They watched the stunning crisp light of dawn break over the horizon in silence; one tiny sun, followed by another, and another, until a cluster of five small white spheres rolled into view, like a flock of angels taking flight.

The bellow of an animal echoed throughout the crags. "That's a Ridgeback," Blink said.

Ducking down, the two boys kept low, scurrying over to the lip of an overhang to scope out what was going on.

Down in the canyon, a troop of mud-soaked Overseers had arrived, mounted on hungry trabasaurs, blast-pikes at the ready.

It wouldn't be long before they picked up the boys' scent.

18

INTO THE RIFT

"I count six. No, wait a second," Blink said quietly, "there's another group coming around from the far side."

Daniel rolled onto his back, searching the sky for a miracle. "We're just going to have to go around them." In a landscape dotted with canyons and mesas, that was easier said than done.

Blink pulled back from the edge. "And run into another patrol coming the other way?"

"Well, we can't outrun 'em. A Ridgeback clocks in at—what?"

Blink hung his head. "As fast as a GoLoader."

"And that's inside a mine," Daniel noted. "Who knows what they can do out in the open." He rolled back onto his belly, taking a last look at the hunting party blockading their route, before crawling safely out of sight.

The two grubs kept low as they ran, hiding behind the occasional outcropping or boulder to get their breath back.

"Least now we know why no one ever came to rescue us from the mines," said Blink. "Look at this place. No one knows we're here."

Everywhere they looked, from the fractured sky to the barren wastes, the sight was the same: total devastation. It would be easy to assume that few people, if any, called this sorry place home.

A little while later they reached a shallow ravine. It took all their effort not to tumble headfirst down into it, but climbing up the opposite slope was worse, sapping energy they couldn't afford to waste. With their dugs soaked in sweat, they crawled to the brow of the hill, only to hear the braying of more Ridgebacks echoing down in the canyon on the other side.

"I told you there'd be another patrol," whispered Blink.

"There are probably patrols everywhere," Daniel whispered back, motioning for Blink to shut up.

For such large animals, the sounds of Ridgebacks padding up the scree were surprisingly light. As they drew closer, the two boys could hear them sniffing the air while the Overseers riding their backs traded that peculiar animalist chatter–

Yach! Yach!

The Ridgeback call, a cross between a roar and a bark, brought the entire patrol to a halt.

It could smell something.

The boys pressed themselves into the dirt; glassy beads of sweat rolled down their faces.

Chatter shot across commlink channels, alerting the other hunting parties to the situation. More Overseers were coming.

Yach! Yach!

Another Ridgeback, a little farther along where the rocky ground had become treacherous and slick with ice, had picked up the scent too. It circled awkwardly back, its feet slipping, before extending its claws and driving them into the ice.

The electrical crackle of blast-pikes igniting came just a moment later.

Though they couldn't see the boys yet, the patrol knew what they had.

Daniel glanced over at Blink. "Run," he said.

Blink looked at him as though that was the craziest thing he'd ever heard. Daniel roared, "Run!"

He jumped up before Blink could say a word, reaching out to the silver relic with his thoughts, the artifact answering his call faster than it had before.

The nearest Ridgeback pulled back its lips to reveal diseased gums and rotting meat stuffed between its dagger-sized teeth. With a snarl, it pounced at Daniel, only to find its way blocked by a swirl of air, a miniature tornado conjured up out of nowhere that the boy was using as a shield. The Ridgeback lunged again, knocking the boy clean off his feet. The Overseer dug in his heels, urging his mount to pin Daniel with its foot–

The spinning vortex shield took care of that, whipping the leg out from under the trabasaur, catching its massive body, and flinging both beast and Overseer at the rest of the pack.

The patrol scattered in chaos, trying not to get hit.

Daniel saw his chance. He scrambled away, his lungs burning in his chest, his teeth aching from the cold. Which way had Blink gone?

Flashes lit up the sky over the next hill. Blast-pikes–Blink . . .

Daniel hustled his way over the rise to find his friend caught between three circling Ridgebacks, Overseers jabbing him in the back every chance they got.

Blink crumpled to his knees.

"Get away from him!" Daniel hollered, whipping his arm back and hurling a vortex from the relic straight at them. The whirlwind smacked one Overseer from his saddle, and rebounded into a second before shooting off into oblivion.

The third Overseer yanked on his Ridgeback's reins, pulling around to face Daniel, holding his blast-pike out ready to strike–and charged right at him.

Daniel ran to help his friend, holding one arm up to block the blow. Electricity flared across the vortex harmlessly, while the Overseer, overshooting his mark, struggled to bring his Ridgeback to halt and turn back around for another pass.

Daniel grabbed his friend by the arm. "Come on!"

Blink groaned, unable to focus. "I can't," he said, breathless. "I can't . . ."

"Get up!"

Plumes of snow blossomed across a distant ridge like smoke, curling behind tiny black specks racing straight for them at blistering speed. More Overseers, more Ridgebacks–more trouble.

Daniel hauled his friend up, wrapping an arm around his shoulders, forcing him to move up the next ridge and beyond–

"It's no use. I'm just slowing you down, Dee," said Blink, trying to shrug him off.

"Just keep going."

"What's the point? Can't you hear 'em breathing? They're right behind us, laughing."

Daniel glanced over his shoulder. Sure enough, the handful of Overseers that Daniel had managed to fend off were back on their mounts, following them slowly just a few paces behind.

Why didn't they attack? What did they know that Daniel and Blink didn't?

He turned back, his breath catching in his throat–"Great . . ."

The two boys teetered on the edge of a cliff. Where the ground sheered away, a vast rift had opened up, exposing the ruins of an ancient city lying half buried in its own destruction.

Above their heads, Nightwatchers circled like vultures, crying, "Who disturbs? Who disturbs?" Behind them, the Overseers slowly moved in.

There was nowhere to go.

"We could jump," Daniel said, clutching the silver relic.

Eyeing the artifact, Blink laughed so hard he coughed up dust. "It's like a mile down. You think you can survive that?"

Daniel wasn't laughing.

"Eighteen-seventy-three and forty-one eighty-two, you are in violation!" an Overseer barked. "Return for processing!"

A Nightwatcher dove down in front of them, forcing them back from the precipice, screeching, "Who disturbs! Who disturbs!"

The two boys raised their hands and turned slowly around. With so many Overseers and Ridgebacks gathering, their run for freedom seemed not only useless, but in some ways ridiculous.

"Get moving!" another Overseer snapped.

The two boys quietly watched each other. Was this it? Was this how it ended? Daniel searched his friend's face, but Blink had a look in his eye that Daniel couldn't quite read.

"Come back for us, Dee," Blink said.

What did that mean? Daniel never got the chance to

ask. Blink rammed his hands into Daniel's chest, pushing him clean over the edge.

Everything moved in slow motion, as though time itself was grinding to a halt–

Nightwatchers flew this way and that, yawping, "Who disturbs! Who disturbs!" Overseers rushed at Blink.

And all the while, Daniel fell backward into the rift, watching his friend Blink Darkada, raising his hands above his head, shouting, "I disturb! I disturb!"

19
FALLEN CITY

Whoosh!

Daniel plummeted, frantically twisting his body, trying to gain some control over his fall–he had to get away from the cliff face before he smashed into it.

Aiming the palm of his hand at the cliff's surface, trying to conjure up the biggest shock wave he could muster in his mind, his whole arm suddenly throbbed from the raw power the silver relic was pumping through it–

Whompff!

The shock wave hit the surface with such force, it gouged molten rock from the cliff's surface before rebounding and propelling Daniel out into the open. With barely enough time to get a sense of where he was falling, he let loose another vortex shield, attempting to cushion the impact.

He fell into the roof of a derelict building, one of the few skyscrapers still standing.

Crashing through the dust, scrambling not to go flying off the other side, he stretched out and grabbed on to whatever he could find, holding on with his fingertips as his body swung out over the edge and slammed down into the cement.

Using all his strength, Daniel dragged himself up onto his elbows, swinging his legs from side to side until he could get a foothold.

Rolling onto the roof, he glanced up. Far, far above him, where Blink had been only a moment ago, a couple of Overseers stood watching. They couldn't reach him down here, but they could signal the Nightwatchers.

Within moments a flock was swooping down to attack.

Daniel needed cover, fast. There had to be somewhere to hide. He peered back over the edge. Beneath him, the husks of once mighty towers lay scattered like hollow dominoes—one had toppled against the skyscraper, its shell smashed open.

Without thinking, Daniel hurled himself off the roof, arms and legs flailing. Hitting the next building with a painful thud, he slid down into its dusty innards. Daylight spilled in through the broken windows, blotted out every now and then by Nightwatchers racing down the outside of the building in an attempt to cut off his escape.

Daniel jammed his heels into the floor, but it barely slowed his fall. The best he could manage was to change direction and slide into a dead end.

He didn't move for the longest time, tears leaving track marks in the dirt on his battered face. Why had Blink done that? Why . . . ?

He lay in the fading light, listening to the Nightwatchers outside yawping to each other, impatient for him to make a move. It was hard to tell how long it had been since dawn, maybe an hour or two, and already it was getting dark again. How fast did this planet spin? Hopefully nighttime out here was equally short.

He'd have to wait them out if he was going to make it anywhere near those ships. He couldn't do it at night. The Nightwatchers had too much of an advantage. Besides, although one or two didn't pose much of a problem now, how was he supposed to take on so many? He wasn't a soldier, he wasn't trained for this; he was just a kid with a superweapon that he barely knew how to operate.

"Who disturbs?" came the distant cries.

"I do," Daniel murmured, curled up into a ball, and, for the first time in what felt like forever, drifted off to sleep.

HIDE-AND-SEEK

A hail of debris showered down from every crack and seam in the roof, wrenching Daniel awake. Something powerful was thundering through the ruins outside, shaking the building to its upended foundations.

Daniel didn't know how long he'd been out. Could have been an hour. Could have been ten. Exhaustion couldn't tell time.

He picked his way over to the nearest smashed-out window, spying a Nightwatcher perched on the head of a crumbling statue. Anyone who didn't know any better would assume it was asleep. They would be wrong. A Nightwatcher never slept; it waited and it watched, just like the others who were out there somewhere right now. Whatever was causing this rumble, they were well used to it.

Wiping down his goggles, Daniel followed the sound over to the other side of the dilapidated tower, scoping out the city through a crack in the outer wall.

A GoLoader with a train of cars several miles long hurtled toward the distant outpost, the same transports he'd ridden down in the mine. The cars, so loaded down that their repulsors barely kept them hovering over the peaks of the ruins, had carved out a well-worn path through the fallen city, a path with buildings tumbled along the route.

As far as Daniel could see, there were maybe a handful of hiding spots between here and there. This was his chance. The way he figured it, so long as he took it slow, and didn't do anything stupid, he stood a good chance of making it.

He just had to stay alive long enough to climb on board. He cupped his hands together, breathing into them. No heat, no gloves, no food, no water–wait . . .

Icicles, hanging down between one or two of the cement seams. He managed to snag one and it stuck to his fingers, but he didn't care. He ran his tongue down the ice like some kind of animal, and when that didn't work, he bit off an end and chewed until his teeth hurt, sucking down the rusty meltwater.

Now to find an exit that didn't lead straight into a trap.

Rubble crunched underfoot as he made his way through the inside of the dilapidated structure, but every time he looked outside, all he could see was flat, exposed ground.

The closest hiding spot on the way to the GoLoader sat about a hundred paces away. The corner of a building had broken off, looking more like a miniature pyramid in the dirt. But it was a long way to go without being spotted. Another potential hideout sat only about twenty paces away, but in the wrong direction. It was anyone's guess if he could find a route from there, but if he didn't decide soon, the rumble from the GoLoader would be gone, and its masking effect on the sound of his footsteps gone along with it–

Daniel jumped down and ran, sprinting for the safety of the closest cover, the shattered remains of a wall. He threw himself to the ground behind it, listening while he caught his breath. . . .

Nothing. No flap of wings. No yawping. They hadn't spotted him. Yet.

Good. Which way now? Behind the wall, some of the inner structure of whatever this building used to be still remained. A partition led down to a sunken section of ground that had obviously been some kind of basement. Jumping down into it, and staying very low, Daniel hugged one edge, following it as far as he could.

And then he ran out of options.

"Surrender, Daniel . . ." whispered a voice, breathing in his ear; the familiar, untrustworthy voice of the Sinja. "There is no shame in giving up."

Daniel jumped out of his skin and spun around. But he was alone.

"I know you hear me," the Sinja persisted, in that awful rasp like grinding metal.

Daniel closed his eyes, refusing to answer.

"There is no use in hiding."

Daniel ground his teeth. He just wanted to scream–

"Or are you too coward to face us?"

He jammed his fingers into his ears to curb the temptation to listen. It didn't help shut the voice up, but at least he had some control. There had to be a way on to that GoLoader, there had to be! No hiding place? Fine, he'd just have to deal with it.

Daniel jumped up and ran faster than he could remember ever running in his life. It was a dumb move.

Twenty paces out and Daniel could already hear Nightwatchers launching from their perches and screaming down his neck. Forty paces out, and he watched his own shadow in the dirt being consumed by the shadow of gigantic wings, swooping in from behind.

Fifty paces out, and its talons were ripping into his shoulders–sixty paces out, and it had him.

Dangling in the air, Daniel kicked his legs, desperate to get it to release him. Instead, another rancorous Nightwatcher shot underneath, grabbing his feet, pecking at him, trying to rip the silver relic from his chest.

With so much extra weight, the first beast sunk its claws deeper into Daniel's shoulders, struggling to stay airborne and make the long, slow turn back toward the mine.

Searing pain shot through Daniel's body, made all the more agonizing by being flown so low over the rumbling GoLoader. He could smell rotting Passava on it.

And all the while, the Sinja laughed in his ear.

Daniel refused to believe this was how it ended.

No, no, no. This was not over!

Struggling to block out the pain, he concentrated purely on the silver relic and the power it was capable of unleashing–

"No!!!" Daniel screamed.

The fury of the tornado that followed was so absolute that for a moment even Daniel could not comprehend the power. Air swirled around them so viciously, it ripped the wings off both Nightwatchers. Howling in agony, the beasts released their grip, and all three tumbled toward the ground–

Slam!

Daniel landed with a thud on the roof of one of the GoLoader cars, holding on to whatever he could find, peering down into the car and finding an Overseer pressed against the opening, staring back.

21

ARMOR OF THE OVERSEERS

Daniel froze, expecting an attack.

But none came.

Why didn't it move?

Or say something?

Wait a minute—this wasn't an Overseer.

This was an empty suit of armor strapped to a pile of identical armored suits, probably recovered from the chamber Daniel had inadvertently unlocked on his way to freedom. The grubs were alive and still working the mines. They must have found these.

He jumped down between two of the cars, clinging to the cages with numb fingers. It wasn't a place anyone was meant to be standing. His feet were planted on two small Fusers, one on each car that kept them magnetically linked to each other. The problem was that each time the GoLoader sped up, or changed direction, they would pull apart, taking Daniel's legs with them, exposing the ruins of the Fallen City speeding by beneath him.

He had to keep reminding himself that he had bigger things to worry about. Every Nightwatcher out here had seen him land on this GoLoader. He had to get out of sight before they figured out an attack. Then there were the Overseers, who were no doubt going to be waiting for him when this rattletrap reached the end of its journey.

Why were they shipping piles and piles of their armor off to who knows where? Heck, what did it matter? The point was, something was getting off this rock–maybe he could go with it. Maybe he'd get lucky and they wouldn't check every car?

Maybe.

With the frigid air whistling past his ears, he tried opening the service hatch on the forward car. It moved a little, but he couldn't get the latch to pop.

He rummaged around in his utility belt. He had to have something he could use–what about this? He pulled out his Regulator. He hadn't seen it since the cave-in.

It had a commlink at one end, which he'd used before. But what else did it do? Oh yeah, it gave off a signal, letting the Overseers know where you were if you got into trouble. Great if you wanted to be found . . .

Or if you wanted to fool somebody.

Daniel held the device up to the side of his head, opening up his socket to activate it. After a moment, he felt a pulse under his fingertips.

High in the sky, a flock of Nightwatchers suddenly changed direction in unison, heading for the GoLoader. Now they really knew where he was.

Daniel smiled to himself. "Thanks, Blink," he whispered, letting the device tumble from his grasp.

The Regulator flipped end over end, disappearing into the chaotic ruins far, far below. A moment later, and the shadows of the Nightwatchers swooped past the GoLoader in their pursuit of a boy they believed had made the insane decision to jump from the train–

The GoLoader lurched into a bend, shifting to a more direct route toward the metal towers of an outpost and the tiny ships supplying the vast freighter hanging above it. With every passing moment, he was a mile or so closer. He didn't have much time.

Daniel checked his pouches again. He had tools, just not very useful ones–wait a minute. This one would do, some kind of impact driver, if he could just wedge the long handle into the latch–there!

Bracing himself against the other car, he kicked at it with everything he had, over and over again–

Bannng! Bannng! Bannng!

The latch flew off, taking the impact driver with it. Daniel tugged at the rusted service hatch. It creaked open, leaving barely enough room for him to squeeze through, but it was all he needed.

With breathing room tight on the inside, it took some maneuvering to climb up onto the bundles of armor. Every time he pushed against another decaying plate, he kicked up enough dust to have to keep coughing it back out. That ruled out hiding in between these things; he'd choke to death before he got anywhere. He snagged one of the helmets–not a perfect solution, but it would keep his airway clear.

"Ouch!" Whoever, or whatever, wore this thing either had the weirdest-shaped head, or loved pain–what were these things all over the inside of the helmet jabbing into his skin?

Daniel tried pulling his head back out, but the helmet had other ideas–

Click.

With the whir of tiny servo motors kicking into gear, a metal probe lashed out from inside the helmet, forcing his skin to peel back to reveal the socket beneath. And then it lunged, into the socket and into his brain.

Daniel's mind exploded with images.

"Noooo!" he screamed, wrestling with the device. Yanking on the connection once, twice, he ripped the probe from his socket and tore off the helmet.

About to cast it aside, he stopped himself. He needed this thing if he was going to blend in. He angled the helmet toward the light and took a look inside. A whole series of probes were waiting for him.

That wasn't happening. He reached inside and started snapping them off one by one.

Outside, the metallic whine of thrusters blotted out all other sound, filling the air with the stench of burning fuel. Pressing up against the vent in the roof, Daniel watched the nose of a worn-out barge swing into view, taking its place in the freight cycle.

The GoLoader had arrived at the outer reaches of the outpost, where gigantic metal platforms teemed with guards. It plowed through the billowing smoke and steam which smothered the industrial wasteland, until after a while a checkpoint emerged from the great noxious clouds–every car was being inspected before it could pass through.

Daniel rooted around for a hiding spot.

He crawled back to the armored suit from which he'd ripped the helmet. There wasn't much space between its breastplate and backplate, but Overseers were a heck of a lot bigger than grubs. It would have to do.

Squeezing his legs into the armor casings, he used his knees to try to pry them apart so he could wriggle in farther, except, what the heck was he caught up on–? This stupid utility belt was going to be the death of him!

The car lurched from side to side. The barge sitting above it had taken control, gearing up for the checkpoint. Ten cars ahead, LightEyes crawled all over the GoLoader, looking for anything suspicious, hopping onward to the next every time the previous one had passed inspection.

Daniel struggled with his buckle–at last! Ripping the utility belt from around his waist, he sandwiched the rest of his body down in between the weathered armor, reaching out and pulling on the helmet at the very last second–

Clank! Clank!

The LightEyes had arrived, crawling around, inspecting his car.

Could they hear him breathing? Everything seemed louder echoing around inside this tin can.

His breath had fogged up the visors. Was that it? Could they see his breath every time they swept their searchlights in his direction?

Should he stop breathing? What was taking them so long? Daniel reached up inside the armor breastplate and carefully pulled his shirt up over his mouth to muffle the sound and hide the steam.

They were going to find him, weren't they? He was dead meat. It was only a matter of time.

Out on a platform, an Overseer barked something unintelligible. There was a loud alarm, and then–nothing.

The car rose gently up into the air on its brief journey to the freighter.

Straightaway, his ears popped as the air pressure changed. Instinctively he wanted to rub the pain away, but if he did that he'd have to take the helmet off and the game would be up, so he just gritted his teeth and suffered through it until the hollow roar of air blasting through the cage began to fade, and he realized he had other problems.

Daniel had trouble catching his breath. The air was so thin up here he was starting to feel dizzy. He gasped, his head bouncing around inside the helmet while he desperately tried sucking down more oxygen–but there wasn't any.

His eyelids fluttered. His strength evaporated. His jumbled thoughts quieted as though he were falling into a deep sleep. But this was not sleep.

On the edge of space, on the edge of freedom, his mind slipped into a terrible blackness.

22

TAKING OUT THE TRASH

Jink. Jink. Joooom.

Daniel had no idea where he was at first. His head pounded, and the cacophonous blare of some kind of alert wasn't helping. He lay on his side, his face all smushed into the helmet. A crust had formed over his eyelids, so it took him a moment to pry them apart. When he did open his eyes, nothing looked as it had before.

How long had he been out this time? How had he gotten out of the car? Come to think of it, where was the car? Where were any of the cars? The entire GoLoader was gone, and most of the armor along with it.

He was in some kind of immense cargo hold that stretched on for miles, its walls dull and metallic. Oily equipment hung on tracks along the ceiling. Massive doors, dented and scratched, studded the walls at regular intervals–

This wasn't like anywhere in the mine. He had to be on that freighter–except the freight was gone. Junked equipment and broken crates littered the deck; some had been swept into neat piles, but there was no one around now, no Overseers, no Nightwatchers.

It was safe to get up, assuming he could get up. He was still curled into a ball inside the Overseer body armor, and–oh, great. He was pinned under a pile of trash.

Gritting his teeth, he struggled to move his arms and legs. Rocking from side to side seemed to help, until–

The shifting junk slid this way and that until what looked to be an unstable part of a compression unit came crashing down on his head with a *BAM!*

Daniel winced, figuring his head was about to cave in, but this Overseer helmet sure could take a beating. Problem was, this compression unit was so heavy, now his head was pinned.

"You have got to be kidding me," he said to no one but himself.

Jink. Jink. Joooom.

What was that? Mixed in with the annoying alert that hadn't stopped since the moment he woke up, a second alarm?

"That can't be good."

It reminded him of a timer. The kind they had on the pulverizers back in the mine to let you know something bad was about to happen.

Daniel didn't want to be around to find out what that something bad was.

He reached over to make sure he still had the silver relic stuck to his chest. He'd warmed up enough he could actually feel with his fingers again—still there. Good.

He just needed a little blast, something to free him up a bit—

Whompff!

The trash heap exploded, sending otherwise immovable junk flying in every direction, broken machine parts embedding along the bulkheads with a *thunk*, *thunk*, *thunk*.

"Oops." Not what he'd had in mind. Oh well. Too late now.

It took a moment or two, since his muscles were sore from being in one position for so long, but eventually Daniel managed to pick himself up off the ground. The armor was so heavy; the Overseers had to be incredibly strong to wear this stuff.

Exhausted, he pulled the helmet off and let it drop to the floor, his hair matted in dried blood where his socket had been pierced by the probe.

He took a moment to catch his breath. The air was different here. He could smell the faint odor that came from the chemicals they coated on electrical circuits—

Jink. Jink. Joooom.

What was that? Trying to figure out what it might be signaling, Daniel eyed a series of five lights above one of the doors: three of them lit, two not.

Daniel stumbled over toward them, his legs still trying

to remember how to work, when the nearest junk pile suddenly got up and started bumbling rapidly toward him.

Daniel's mouth hung open, a dim light shining on a corner of his mind as a memory came forth.

"Enginoid . . ." he said. "You're an enginoid. . . ." He remembered! He couldn't quite put his finger on where he'd seen one, but he knew he'd seen them before.

This one, all worn out save for a few scratched-up lime-green markings, came straight at him, sweeping up the trash. Daniel held his hands up. "I . . . I don't want any trouble," he said.

As robots go, it appeared harmless enough, tottering like a small child, taking a few bouncy steps in between rests, but Daniel didn't want to provoke it. Who knew what else it was programmed for?

"I just need help," he added, taking another step back, the robot edging closer.

What was it about enginoids that he needed to remember? Something important.

The enginoid dithered before rumbling toward him faster than before.

"Please?"

Jink. Jink. Joooom.

Another light went on above the door. Daniel wagged an accusing finger, refusing to get out of the way. "What does that mean?" he said. "That has to mean something–"

Three paces, two paces, one . . .

Hissss, kthunk, kthunk kthunk!

The enginoid went to pieces–literally–breaking apart into twenty or thirty individual fragments, each one with a mind of its own. They rolled around Daniel like a school of fish trying to avoid a shark.

Daniel sidestepped, trying to get out of their way, but blocking the path of one of the smaller ones. It beeped in annoyance before rolling around him.

"Oh, right . . ."

Enginoids weren't one robot; they were a bunch of robots working together–and these ones weren't sticking around. Reconfiguring themselves back into a single unit, the enginoid was already halfway across the hangar.

Daniel ran after it. "Where do I go?" he insisted. "What do I do?"

An almighty rumble erupted near the ceiling. Daniel glanced up to see thick gigantic doors thundering down, releasing tons more garbage down into the hangar all around him. What looked like the front half of an entire ship came crashing down not more than a few paces away.

"Hey, wait for me!" Daniel cried.

The enginoid had opened up a compartment in the bulkhead and was getting itself situated inside. The door started to close.

"Hey!" Daniel jammed his foot in the gap. Not the best idea; he wedged his shoulder in quick before he didn't have much of a foot left.

The enginoid extended an arm, but instead of helping out, it poked him in the ribs, trying to get him to leave.

Angrily, Daniel squeezed through. "What is your problem?" he said, the door hammering shut behind him.

Despite the fact that the compartment was so snug they were jammed up against each other, cheek to cheek, the enginoid wouldn't look him in the eye.

Jink. Jink. Joooom–

Out in the cargo hold, hazard lights flared, a faint hiss grew into a roar, metal junk slid across the deck, and then–*pop!*

The deck opened up, thrusting the pile of trash Daniel had just been in out into the vacuum of a very crowded area of space.

A planet-sized ball of smog the color of disease sat ringed with trash. In front of it, a hulking great garbage boat slid silently beneath the cargo hold. Daniel could make out the words "beg ration" on its side.

Daniel turned to the robot. "I could have died out there!"

Tiny hatches flipped open on each one of the individual units, revealing thirty or so sets of visual sensors, each one scrutinizing him nervously.

"Yeah, you should feel bad," said Daniel.

The trembling hatches snapped shut in unison.

Out in space, the boat, far from ready for the rain of junk hammering down on it, rolled slowly over, trying to avoid any major damage, but it wasn't a ship designed for fancy flying.

"Hold! Hold! Hold!" a tinny voice cried.

Daniel glanced up at the tiny amplifier buried in a control panel in the ceiling.

"I got Debriss on comms," said another over the speaker "They are not happy–"

Daniel guessed that had to make sense to somebody, just not to him. Pretty soon a whole bunch of voices were arguing with one another–ordinary voices from regular people.

"Who in the name of Jirrot's Thistle authorized this dump?" one of them yelled.

The unnaturally calm response silenced everybody. "We have a schedule to keep. I will not miss this rendezvous."

Daniel didn't recognize the voice, but he sure didn't trust it. Asking for help would have to wait. He turned to the enginoid. "How long to the next planet?" he asked.

But the enginoid was busy extending an arm, reaching up to activate one of the controls on the ceiling. The whole compartment shuddered before lurching through a series of shafts. When the door rolled open, a conveyor belt stretched down a long, dark corridor filled with pipes and tubes and the occasional dim light.

The enginoid shuffled onto the belt, collapsing down into a small misshapen block as it was carried away. With nowhere else to go, Daniel cautiously tagged along. Around the bend, steam vented from the occasional nozzle, making everything slick with moisture.

"Where are we going?" Daniel asked, even though he knew by now that the enginoid wasn't about to reply.

From the depths of another shadowy recess, a door

rolled open and out waddled a different type of enginoid. Behind it, a third one slithered down from a hatch in the ceiling. The snakelike oddity gave Daniel the most curious look before coiling itself up and shutting down.

When the belt had filled up with every type of enginoid imaginable, it conveyed them into a final chamber and rolled the door shut behind them. The air, thick with the reek of acid, burned in Daniel's throat.

What was this place? He clambered over to a small hatch and peered through the observation glass. A control booth sat on the other side, with a sign in large lettering that read:

WARNING, ACID SHOWER, KEEP CLEAR.

The rumble of liquids priming in the nozzles filled the chamber.

Daniel pounded on the glass. "Let me out! Somebody help! Let me out of here!"

At the end of the chamber, one by one, the showerheads began pumping acid, spraying each and every enginoid–

"Help me! Somebody–!"

Shoom!

The hatch rolled open. Without thinking, Daniel leapt out into the booth, collapsing in a heap on the deck, gasping for clean air. "Thank you," he wheezed. The reply that came back consisted of a series of clicks and tiny grumbles.

Daniel recognized it as such, but for some reason he could actually understand it.

His rescuer had said, "Are you mad? You could have

gotten yourself killed! How did you end up in there?"

Daniel sat up, but there didn't appear to be anyone else in the room. "I didn't know where I was going," he explained.

The disapproving clicks and grumbles that came back in response translated as "Well, aren't you just a few rungs short on the evolutionary ladder. Your parents must be very proud."

Daniel struggled onto his feet. That wasn't coming from any amplifier. Whoever he was talking to was in the room. But where? "If I knew who my parents were, I'd ask them," he said. Pipes, grilles, vents, electrical panels–he had to be hiding somewhere.

"Up here, genius."

At the edge of the room, near the ceiling right at the rim of a maintenance shaft, a small, twitching nose poked out, sniffing the air. Glowing light-wire whiskers bristled around its snout. What emerged from the shadows was a rather odd-looking creature that reminded Daniel of a drote in a fur coat.

Daniel stood his ground. "What are you?" he asked.

"What am I?" the creature replied. "I'm a rat," he said. "What else would I be?"

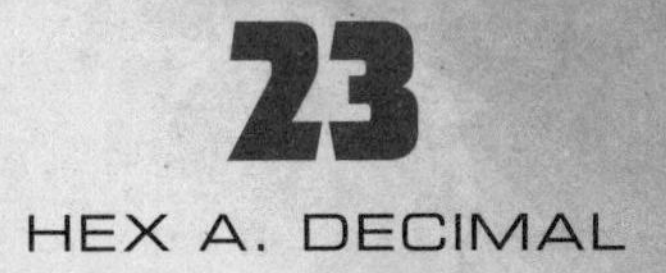

23
HEX A. DECIMAL

"You can speak," said Daniel, surprised.

"You understand Mendese," the rat replied, with suspicion. "No human speaks Mendese."

"Mendese?"

"The anatom language," the rat explained, darting along a conduit to get a better look at him.

Daniel didn't recognize the word. "What's an anatom?" he asked, putting a little distance between himself and the rat, just in case it decided to attack.

"What's an anatom?" said the rat, sounding genuinely shocked. "Where have you been living, under a rock?"

"Pretty much."

"An anatom is–well–like me!" He threw his little paws up in a gesture closely mimicking human exasperation.

"So you're an animal?"

"How dare you! I'm not an animal."

"You might want to check a mirror."

"I look like an animal. I am not an actual animal, like you." He rapped his knuckles on one of his shiny back legs. "Look at that. Real titanium. Used to be part of a vacuum cleaner. Not anymore. Do you know any other rats with titanium legs? Thought not. There's *Rattus cyberneticus*, and then there's me, a cut above. The ultimate rat. Pinnacle of rat existence. Without me the universe would cease to function."

"I see," said Daniel, giving the control booth a little tour. There wasn't much to it; most of it appeared automated. A series of panels operated the valves, pumping acid into the showers. The corporation that made the acid was very proud of the fact that its product killed 99 percent of all living things; it was printed so many times on the huge tanks, it looked at first like a decorative pattern. "So what do you do that's so important?"

"What do I do?"

"Apart from repeat all my questions."

"Repeat all your questions?" The rat pulled himself up onto his hind legs, smoothing down the fur on the top of his head in an effort to make himself more presentable. "Well," he said, "I'm the, er, ruler of the galaxy, obviously."

Daniel had never heard anything more ridiculous in his life. At least, as far as he could remember of his life, but he was happy to play along if it got him out of here. "And do you have a name, or should I just call you your majesty?"

The rat sighed, his ears flopping down. "You don't believe me."

There was the exit. Daniel headed straight for it. "Nope," he said.

The rat called after him, the seriousness in his voice something Daniel hadn't heard before now. "My name is Hex A. Decimal, and I am one hundred and sixty-seven years old," the rat proclaimed proudly, his whiskers twinkling. "For every star that has a planet, I've been to nearly all of them. I've met Kakaridans as tall as trees, and seen Tantaurees leap a hundred paces on worlds where you would barely be able to walk. I have seen many things, human, and I know a stowaway when I see one."

Daniel stood frozen in his tracks. What could he possibly say to that? He couldn't bring himself to turn around. Thinking quickly, he tried to sound confident when he said over his shoulder, "How do you know I don't work here?"

"Because I work here." Good point.

"Not as many *Xenopsylla cheopis* on me as you assumed, eh, human?"

"Xenop-what?"

"Fleas," proudly explained the rat. "I don't have any."

Everybody in the mines caught fleas at one time or another. It was just part of life. Daniel wasn't sure he understood why this rat was so pleased by the fact he'd managed to lose a few.

Jumping down from the conduit, the rat scurried around in front him, blocking his exit. "Who are you and what are you doing on my ship?" he said, his face hard and serious, which was an impressive feat for a fur-covered rodent. "The truth, human, before I alert the securities."

Enough games. Standing his ground, Daniel looked the rat right in the eye. "My name is Daniel Coldstar," he said between gritted teeth. "I am a fugitive from the relic mines. I have lived under the boot of the Overseers my entire life. I will not go back–and I will defend myself."

Pulling his arm back, Daniel created the first whisper of a luminous vortex shield, lighting up the eyes of the rat.

For his part, Hex A. Decimal's mouth hung open as he caught sight for the very first time of the silver relic pinned to Daniel's chest.

Mustering all the shock and awe that a rodent's face was capable of, he returned Daniel's gaze.

"An Aegis?" said Hex. "You're a Truth Seeker!"

24

STAR CHARTS OF THE *WAKEENEE*

Just the sound of the name Truth Seeker had Daniel's attention. The reverence it brought to the rodent's face, however? Now that really had his skin prickling.

Whoever these Truth Seekers were, they clearly held powerful significance. Daniel hadn't made any promises when he'd left that he would find help and free everyone from the mines, but maybe these Truth Seekers could make it happen.

Hex edged closer, showing far more respect toward Daniel now. "Are you on a secret mission?"

Daniel lowered his arm, letting the shield evaporate, but kept his mouth shut. If passing himself off as one of these Truth Seekers was going to get him the help he needed, he was happy to do it, but the surest way to let this rat know that he didn't know what the heck he was talking about was to open his mouth.

"You're a long way from home, Truth Seeker," said the rat, running circles around him, inspecting Daniel from top to bottom. "You're on your own out here."

"I don't even know where here is," said Daniel.

"Where are you trying to get to?"

"I don't know."

Prodding him with a steel claw, the rat said, "You know, I'd assumed you Truth Seekers were a little more on top of things. But then again, I've never seen one up close. I didn't know you were all so young. What are you, like, twelve?"

"Stop it!" Daniel slapped his paw away. "I am not twelve years old!" Any idiot could see that, except this rat, it seemed.

"Then how old you are?"

"Older than twelve."

"By how much?"

"I don't know."

"About a week?"

"More than a week."

"Don't know where you are. Don't know where you're going. Don't know how old you are–"

"Because of this!" Daniel snapped, angrily exposing the socket buried in his temple. "They wiped my memory. All our memories. I think it's malfunctioning. Some of it's coming back–just bits and pieces."

Watching Daniel's skin slowly peel away from the embedded device, the baffled rodent jumped up onto his shoulder for a closer inspection, his light-wire whiskers tickling the boy's ear.

"Well, that's a first," the rodent replied, completely baffled. "I've never seen a human with one before. You and I aren't so different after all." Hex leapt onto the nearest pipe running along the wall at eye level, parting the fur behind one of his ears, exposing a socket no wider than a pinkie finger buried in his head. "See? It's a Z eighty-two. Latest model," the rat bragged. "They put them on the likes of me. Not a human."

"You still haven't told me what an anatom is," said Daniel.

"Engineered servants. Part living being, part machine."

"I am human," Daniel protested.

"Are you sure about that–?"

Suddenly they both heard the loud clanking of boots on the deck outside the door.

"I wouldn't be around when he gets here, if I were you," Hex suggested, scampering from pipe to conduit on his way back up to the maintenance shaft. "They don't like Truth Seekers on this ship. Bad for business."

Daniel rushed over to the door, activating the lock controls.

"Hey, who's in there?" a muffled voice complained from outside, pounding on the door. "Open up!"

Daniel backed away, praying it didn't fly open.

The rat put his steely finger up to his mouth, making a shushing sign. Then he whispered, "It's on a time release. It's a safety thing; vent the gases. Anyway, nice meeting you–"

Wait! Daniel silently mouthed. No matter where he looked, there really was nowhere else to go except back into the acid shower. He looked at Hex while raising his hands up to his shoulders as if to say, "Where do I go?"

The rat loitered at the entrance to the maintenance shaft, a slow thought drifting across his artificial eyes. "I'll make you a deal."

Exasperated, Daniel said, "What kind of deal?"

"I know ways of getting around this ship that'll keep you hidden for months," he said, cleaning his fur. "Just promise to take me with you when you get to where you're going."

Daniel didn't see that as much of an issue at all. So this rat wanted to tag along? Who cares? "Fine!" he said, shrugging.

Hex nodded, satisfied. "Well, get climbing, genius. It's this way into the maintenance tunnels. I just hope you fit."

Over at the door, the control panel began chirping out a stream of beeps–maybe the timer was up, or maybe the crewman outside had set off the override. Either way, Daniel was gone. Scrambling up the conduit, he shimmied into the maintenance tunnel, headfirst, pulling his feet through just in time.

The hatch slammed shut just as the door to the booth rolled open.

Hex put a tiny steel claw to his mouth, warning Daniel to stay quiet.

Together they listened to the operator storming inside.

"Ugh, cheese on rice . . ." the operator grumbled. A moment later, the click of a comm channel opening. "*WaKeenee* tower? Shutting down number three. Looks like an enginoid bailed on its shower. Got an open hatch and acid everywhere. I'll be back in ten, let me suit up."

Making extra sure that the operator was actually gone, Hex nodded for Daniel to follow. "Come on."

Daniel crawled after him as fast as he could manage, even though the narrow shaft barely gave him room enough to move his shoulders. At every intersection, the rat would keep scampering ahead to make sure the coast was clear before leading him off in another direction. It took forever.

"You know, you might not be twelve," the rat mused. "If you're not using standard galactic time. If you were from Tantara, that planet takes so long to roll around its sun, you'd be three. Skepsis moves so fast you'd be one hundred and eight. I've met enough humans in my time to know that in galactic standard time, you look twelve. I say stick with twelve until we find out otherwise."

"Okay! I don't really care! Can we just get some fresh air, I'm dying back here."

Hex refused. "Can't risk it," he said. "The *WaKeenee* is very small for a merchant vessel," the rodent explained over and over. "She's just a hundred and twenty-eight miles long, fifteen miles deep and only has a little under three thousand decks."

That sounded like a lot of space to hide in to Daniel. "What about the crew?"

"A crew of seventy, so you're bound to run into somebody. You know what I'm saying?"

Daniel had no idea what he was saying; his estimates sounded way off, but what did he know? "Okay, I'll stay out of sight. What about the cargo?" he asked with a grunt. His elbows were sore and his back ached. They had to stop sooner or later.

"What about it?"

"I hid in a GoLoader, filled with armor–relic armor. When I woke up, all the cars were gone. I was in a junk pile," Daniel explained.

"So what?" said Hex, clearly not understanding the significance.

"So where did you pick me up from? Where did it all go? There has to be a list somewhere–a manifest."

"Beats me, kid."

Daniel refused to go any farther.

The rat stopped in his tracks and turned around. Even if you couldn't speak Mendese, the tone of the rapid-fire clicks would have gotten the point across. "Kid, we're out on the front range, hauling to and from a thousand different worlds. We pick up from planets, stations, and other ships. We don't care what it is, where it came from, or where it's going. We don't care if it's even legal. We don't. Ask. Questions."

Daniel exploded. "Well, somebody had to know what was on board! They combed through everything pretty thoroughly–"

Hex threw his paws over Daniel's mouth in a panic. "Will you be quiet?" He waited for Daniel to catch his breath and calm down. "It's standard procedure. The receiver checks for transit damage, files a claim with their insurer, and we take out the trash. It's all part of the service."

Daniel wouldn't give up. "What about the Truth Seekers? Don't they have a planet?"

Hex narrowed his eyes. "Wait a minute. . . ." he clicked. "They?"

"I meant we. Don't we have a planet somewhere?"

Hex did not seem convinced. "You're not a very good liar."

Daniel shrugged. "That's because I'm only used to telling the truth."

Hex chewed on that thought for a moment. "Huh. Good point. Kid," he said, "Truth Seekers operate on half the planets in the galaxy. Running into one ain't going to be hard."

"Then why have you never seen one?"

"Because most of my adventures happen while I'm hiding."

"Okay, so where's the nearest planet where we'll find one?"

"Questions, questions! Sheesh, kid, I don't know!"

"I thought you knew everything."

"I don't have time to know everything," said the rat, his light-wire whiskers twitching indignantly. "It's a very large universe and I'm a very busy rodent. Look at all these wires. They don't chew through themselves, you know," he said, before stopping himself. "Hmm," Hex mused. "I wonder. Wait here," he said, shooting off down the tunnel.

Daniel was happy to oblige; he had no intention of going anywhere. Resting his head on his arms, he waited patiently while the rat gathered what he needed from a supply pouch and started chewing through a heavy-duty conduit. Pulling out a cable, he gnawed it in half, inserted a T-junction, and ran a line from it all the way back down to Daniel.

Attaching a jack to the end of the line, he said, "If you're wired up to a socket, that must mean you can be programmed just like I can–"

"I'm not an anatom!"

"You know what I mean." He held up the finished connector. "The *WaKeenee*'s navigation system."

"I'm not sure that's a good idea," Daniel remarked, edging backward.

Hex wouldn't take no for answer. Pleased with his ingenuity, he leapt onto Daniel's head, poking his little steel claws around the tiny opening, and buried the jack into the socket.

"Hey!" Daniel protested, but it was too late. A blue streak of electricity shot out of his head, knocking Hex to the ground.

With his brain vibrating around inside his head, Daniel clutched his skull, holding on tight in case it came bouncing out through his ears. Stars burst across the inside of his eyeballs, each searing pinprick a star system complete with names, orbits, hazards, shipping lanes–

Screaming in abject agony, Daniel ripped the cable from his socket and collapsed.

Hex watched him for the longest time, a motionless heap in the maintenance shaft. He held a paw over his mouth. "Oh no, I think I've killed him." But it was a short-lived execution.

Daniel took a sharp breath, holding his head up, trying to focus on the rat. The overwhelming mosaic of information and emotion took an eternity to process. He held out his hand as though begging it to stop, and when Hex shuffled closer to see what he could do to help, Daniel grabbed him by the throat and snatched him up to his face.

"Never. Do that. Again . . ." he growled.

"I was only trying to help," croaked Hex.

Daniel threw the anatom back down the shaft, pushing himself up on to unsteady knees. He took a moment to catch his breath.

"Musa Degh," Daniel said eventually. "All I can see is a planet called Musa Degh."

Hex's whiskers lost all their sparkle. "Musa Degh?" he said, perplexed. "That's impossible. I don't think that planet even exists anymore."

25

DOUBLE CROSS ON THE FRONT RANGE

Hex rubbed his furry little neck. “Ah, kid,” he said, apologetically. “I obviously scrambled your brain. Give it time–I’m sure it’ll clear right up in a day or two, maybe a week.”

“What do you mean?” asked Daniel.

Hex tried on a sheepish smile, but it didn’t quite fit his face. “Okay,” he admitted. “You got me. Maybe a month. If you still have problems after that, I’d go see somebody. I’m really sorry. Really.”

Daniel rolled his eyes. “Not that. The planet. How can it not exist?”

“That’s what you’re worried about?”

“Yes.”

“Huh.” With obvious relief, the rat turned around and got going again, signaling Daniel to keep following. “A planet can disappear for all kinds of reasons. Maybe its star went supernova, or something crashed into it. I can't remember what happened to this one, it was over a hundred years ago. If I remember, I think it got destroyed in the last war."

"The last war . . . ?" What was it the Overseers were always telling them? *Your efforts in the war will be rewarded.*

"We're not still at war?"

"Somebody's always at war with somebody," Hex remarked, leading Daniel up into a junction compartment, a noisy hole filled with wires, pipes, and relays.

A handful of maintenance shafts branched off in various directions. Hex quickly set about closing a few of them off.

"You'll be okay in here for a while," said the rat, jabbing a tiny paw at the hatch above Daniel's head. "Just don't open that. Stay put, and I'll get you a blanket or something."

As hideouts go, this one seemed like a pretty safe bet. At least Daniel had room to get up and stretch in. "Thank you," he said.

Hex shrugged. "Good for a couple days."

"What about food?"

Hex looked to the heavens, exasperated. "There's always something."

Daniel shrugged. "I have to eat. I'm starving."

"All right! I'll figure something out."

The rat climbed into another shaft, but Daniel wasn't done. "Why is Musa Degh still on the charts, if it was destroyed?" he asked.

Hex glanced over his shoulder. "It's not."

"Then why is my brain telling me it's important? Are there Truth Seekers there, or is it where I got on board–"

"What? No! Kid, I don't know where you got on board, but if anything of that planet still exists, we're nowhere near it and never have been. The Embers are over a thousand light-years from here."

"Then why do I know its name . . . ?"

"You got a short in the socket," Hex replied, holding out a paw as though he were training a pet. "Now, stay . . . stay." Satisfied that Daniel wasn't about to go anywhere, Hex darted off down the shaft.

Daniel sank to the deck, head in his hands; so many questions with no obvious answers. If the relic mines weren't on Musa Degh, what was he remembering? His home? Was he born there? Not possible; Musa Degh was destroyed a century ago–that'd make Daniel over a hundred years old. Not possible! Besides–

What was that smell?

His stomach growled, saliva washing through his mouth–deep-fried yampa with sliced pipiril. Real food. Somewhere in the back of his brain a memory was being dragged out, kicking and screaming. Yampa and pipiril, usually served with some kind of roast thing on a stick that dripped grease down your chin every time you bit into it.

Daniel hadn't eaten in days; no way was he staying put. He followed his nose. The aroma wafted in through the air vents surrounding the hatch in the ceiling–the very place Hex had warned him not to go. What the heck was up there? Could be a canteen. Could be a private room. There was no way of knowing unless he looked.

He pressed his ear to the metal hatch. He couldn't hear anyone walking around, but that didn't mean anything.

Daniel glanced back down the open maintenance shaft. No sign of the rat.

Did he dare risk it? His head told him not to be so stupid, but his head wasn't in charge right now–his every impulse had been rerouted through his stomach.

He unlocked the hatch, too impatient to let it finish retracting before poking his head out.

There was no food; just a trick of the air duct.

Whoever had just served themselves up a meal could have been at the other end of the ship, for all it mattered.

Daniel had popped his head up in the middle of the landing strip of a massive hangar. At the far end a whole bunch of the *WaKeenee*'s crew were gathered together, watching a ship gliding in through the hangar doors, passing right over Daniel's head–

THRUMMMMMMMM!

The thick smoke of maneuvering thrusters fired relentlessly down on Daniel, choking off his air and stinging his eyes. It was only at the last possible moment, and through heavy tears, that he noticed the landing gear extending out through the fog, coming straight at him–

He ducked down just in time, the whole deck shuddering as the weighty vessel finally came to rest.

Sucking down clean air from the ducts, Daniel listened to the whine of servo motors extending the boarding ramps, the hiss of pressure equalizing, and the rumble of the vessel's airlock opening.

He poked his head back up to see the back of a tall figure stepping down onto the flight deck, cloaked in scavenged parts.

A single member of the crew stepped forward to meet him, wearing a long greatcoat fastened up around the neck, with a sidearm holstered at the shoulder.

Daniel recognized his unnaturally calm voice immediately as the one he'd heard when he first woke up in the cargo hold: the captain of the *WaKeenee.* "You're late," he said.

In a dialect of Jarabic that Daniel could barely understand, the visitor replied, "I don't care. Do you have it?"

The captain of the *WaKeenee* held out a small device to the visitor, sleek and silver. "Your payment," he said. "The rest of the ship is yours. Just make it look like a leecher attack."

"Not a problem," said the visitor, signaling his ship. "I brought actual leechers."

All at once, awkward-shaped figures began shambling down the boarding ramps.

"Your crew has ten minutes to abandon ship. I make no guarantee of their safety after that."

With a satisfied nod, the captain strode away. "Oh, my employer expects all evidence that his cargo was ever aboard this ship to be extinguished."

Panic broke out among the assembled crew. One of them lunged at their commander. "Captain, what are you doing? This ain't the plan!"

The visitor launched a projectile at the crewman, a slimy, black parasite with metal teeth rotating from inside a single sucker. Boring into the back of his neck, the crewman struggled against the leecher, but it was a losing battle. The parasite emitted a translucent holographic shell, enveloping its victim.

In mere seconds, life left the crewman's eyes, slipping from that of a thinking, feeling human into that of a dead automaton, a zombie whose every thought and action were dictated by the parasite. With the transformation complete, the crewman joined the other leechers in attacking his own shipmates.

Daniel was absolutely okay with running away. Scrambling back down inside the junction compartment, he scratched around for the controls to close the hatch–

Where were they?

WHERE WERE THEY?

There!

He reached up to the panel above his head–only to have a fetid hand reach down inside and grab him before he could throw the switch.

The leecher yanked him off his feet.

Daniel kicked and wrestled against its grasp, but the nightmare was only beginning.

The leecher's face emerged, just inches from his own: a ghostly, translucent one. And the more Daniel looked into its eyes, the more he realized that this face was merely a mask, a holocule stretched over the rotting flesh of a dead victim whose body it used as a vehicle for the attack.

26
LEECHERS!

In the palm of the leecher's free hand, a glistening, slime-covered parasite slithered toward Daniel's neck, its razor-sharp teeth whirring away.

Daniel grabbed the leecher's wrist with everything he had, trying to push it away.

Down below, a muffled tirade of angry clicks and hisses erupted from under a blanket emerging from one of the shafts. It translated roughly as: "I told you, don't open that hatch!" but Daniel was pretty sure if his Mendese vocabulary had been bigger, it would have been far more colorful.

Hex threw the blanket aside and ran up Daniel's leg.

"I thought I could smell food!" Daniel explained, barely able to breathe.

"From an air duct? How have you not died from

stupidity before now? It could have come from anywhere!" Hex scolded, scrambling over Daniel's back and perching on his shoulder.

"So I discovered!" Daniel yelped, rapidly losing his struggle with the leecher. "Are you going to help or just sit there?"

Hex shivered, watching the slithering parasite edge closer. "Ugh, I hate these things." And with that he leapt over onto the leecher's hand, biting down on the parasite and flinging it away before jumping back to relative safety, using Daniel as a springboard and somersaulting up to the control panel, hitting the switch with a click.

The hatch slammed shut on the leecher's arm, forcing it to loosen its grip.

Daniel landed in a heap, Hex running circles around him, opening up all the access panels to the shafts. "We have to find somewhere to hide."

"It's no use, they'll hunt us down," Daniel explained, coughing for air. "We've been sold out. Your captain told them not to leave any survivors."

"I knew he was no good the moment they hired him," Hex replied, climbing up to survey the tunnel closest to the deck, ducking out of the way of the leecher's hand.

Shaped like a trench, this shaft ran along the deck, separated from the surface by grates every few paces, flight-deck lights shining down through the mesh. "A front-row seat, but we don't have a choice. Come on, human."

Hex didn't wait around to see if Daniel would follow. Pressing flat to the shadows, the anatom ducked down onto all fours and scurried beneath the lowest pipes, following their length down the access trench.

Daniel tried to keep up, but it was hopeless. With a human body shape, he just couldn't do the things a rat could do. Hex could push his bones together to squeeze through holes as small as his head–all Daniel could do was get stuck.

Hex tossed an impatient look over his shoulder. "Try going around, genius."

High above their heads, a wailing siren erupted with an earsplitting screech. Weapons fire shot back and forth across the flight deck, lighting up the smoke rolling in from all sides–

Slam!

A *WaKeenee* crewman landed on the grate, his clothes ripped and bloodied, a leecher bearing down on him, looking like rotten flesh encased in jelly.

Daniel held his breath, watching in horror as the leecher gripped the man's head, pressing his face tight against the grille–slapping a parasite on the back of his neck.

Holocules spread rapidly over the victim's skull, encasing him within moments, choking off his air until a new face emerged, and a new personality–

Sick to his stomach, Daniel couldn't watch anymore. He bolted into the darkness in search of Hex.

"What are they doing to those people?" he said.

"Leeching!" Hex replied, yanking a panel off the wall, scratching around inside for a particular conduit. "What does it look like?"

"I don't understand!" Daniel said.

"They're Umbrian nomads," Hex explained, as though that explained anything. Finally, he pulled the correct wire from the conduit and patched into it with his tail. His ears flattened against his head. "Oh no . . ." he said.

"What is it?"

"All commlinks are offline and somebody disabled the distress signal. We're on our own," said the rat, disconnecting from the cable and getting right in Daniel's face. "If you're just pretending that you're all screwy in the head, or you still have some secret Truth Seeker trick up your sleeve, now would be the time to use it."

Daniel didn't know what to say. He shrugged apologetically. "There has to be a way out of this."

Hex thought long and hard. "There is if you can keep us both alive long enough to get there," he said. "But you weren't doing too well against that leecher–"

"It took me by surprise," Daniel explained, his jaw set in defiance. "It won't happen again."

"I hope not, because I'm just a rat, kid. I'm no good in a fight."

Daniel figured that was a fair observation. "So where do we need to get to?"

"We're already here," Hex explained. "The flight deck has its own set of escape pods. We just need to reach one."

"Assuming they haven't disabled those too?"

Hex didn't answer. He'd obviously been thinking the same thing.

Daniel scooted forward. "Come on," he said. "Let's go."

Hex held him back. "Don't be so quick to die, kid. You hear that war out there? Let's wait it out."

Easier said than done. When the air wasn't filled with the din of weapons fire, or the shouts and screams of pitched battle, the *WaKeenee* shrieked every time her hull was ripped open.

Daniel shut his eyes to it, but it didn't help. Staying holed up in the trench went against everything he believed in. "We should be helping them," he muttered.

"Don't be so naïve. They wouldn't be helping you," said the rat.

"What are those creatures anyway?"

"The leechers? Umbrian nomads."

"No, not the people, the parasites."

"Those are the people," Hex explained.

Daniel was pretty sure that the anatom didn't know what he was talking about. "Those aren't humans. They're slugs."

"Now. Five thousand years ago they looked just like you, kid. Until their world was destroyed," he said. "The survivors wandered the galaxy looking for a new home. When that got destroyed, they gave up on planets and decided to become permanent themselves. They created those parasites out of biocomputers and downloaded their minds into them. Now they just move from body to body, sucking all the life out of it, until it's time to move on to the next one."

Daniel was disgusted, but impressed at the rat's lesson.

"I'm over a hundred and sixty-seven years old, kid. That, and I'm plugged into the ship's computer."

It was hard to say how long it really took for the sound of fighting to give way to deafening silence, but when it came, it was perhaps the most unnerving thing of all.

Hesitantly, Daniel pressed his face up against one of the grates, trying to get a look at the situation on the flight deck.

"I think they're gone," he whispered.

Hex didn't need to look; his nose twitched. "No, they're still out there somewhere," he said, releasing the locking clips on the grate. "I can smell them. Wait here," he said, and shot out onto the flight deck in a blinding burst of speed.

With no sign of leechers anywhere, Daniel poked his head up to watch Hex scurrying past the landing gear of the visiting ship. The rat paused to sniff the air; still no leechers. Before long he'd made it all the way over to the far bulkhead.

He gave Daniel the all-clear signal.

Daniel slid the grate to one side and climbed on out.

Creeping over to join Hex, the eerie quiet of the abandoned landing bay set every survival instinct he had on fire. He couldn't figure out from where–but he had the distinct feeling he was being watched.

"Stay close," Hex whispered, running ahead toward a series of angled hatches buried in a line of depressions down the side of the deck–the escape pods.

Hex jumped across to the control pad while Daniel stood watch. "Locked out," he said, not remotely surprised. He plugged the end of his tail into the panel's data socket and started swishing it around. "Just a warning: if I light up like a Jooshee, something went wrong."

"What's a . . ."

Hex waited, but Daniel didn't say anything else. "Are you going to finish that sentence? Why is your mouth hanging open like a flytrap?"

Daniel nodded at the open hangar doors. Out in space, a tiny object glinted in the starlight. Was that another ship? Daniel wondered. Seemed awfully small, but what did he know? One thing was for certain: it was coming their way. "Hurry up, will you? It's about to get crowded in here."

Still oddly swishing his rear end around, Hex yelled, "You do it if you think you can do a better job!"

Click.

"Yes!"

With a loud clunk, the door to the escape pod rolled open, only to reveal a leecher waiting for them!

Hex hissed at the creature, exposing a set of razor-sharp teeth. Before the leecher could even react, Hex flew at it, sinking his teeth into the parasite on the back of its neck and ripping it off.

The leecher collapsed, its holocule shell evaporating, leaving nothing but a corpse and a slime-covered parasite, stuck wriggling on its back.

Clunk. Clunk. Clunk.

All down the line, the escape pods opened up like prison cells, releasing leecher after leecher.

Daniel spun around, not sure which way to turn, with leechers coming at him from every direction and that small ship, or object, or whatever the heck it was, blasting into the hangar on a trajectory aimed straight at him.

On pure impulse, Daniel fired up the silver relic.

Whompff!

"Stay close!" he yelled. "I can protect you!"

"You tell me this now?!" Hex's clicks were firing so rapidly, they were almost a screech.

A leecher had him; legs in one hand, body in the other, stretching the little anatom taut.

"Leave him alone!" Daniel cried.

The leecher didn't care. It ripped the titanium legs off the rat and tossed the pieces aside.

In that moment, rage so engulfed Daniel that he couldn't think straight. Tears spilled from his eyes, and all thought of using the silver relic to defend himself vanished.

Through gritted teeth, he snarled, "Come and get me!"

They never got the chance; what had flown into the hangar was not a ship, or a drone, or some kind of weapon–but a person.

Clad in some kind of sleek, armored kilt, and with a shock of red hair, she arrived like a fireball, stripping the deck of its plating, ripping panels from the bulkheads, bending the seemingly immovable to her will.

She landed so gently that she made barely a sound, though the debris she had brought with her rattled like a GoLoader, swirling around them, forming an impenetrable shield.

"You have no authority here, Truth Seeker!" one of the leechers rasped through desiccated vocal cords.

She grimaced. "Oopsies," she said, "I was afraid you were going to say that." And with a single thought she unleashed the most destructive assault Daniel had ever seen. With one massive *WHOMPFF!* the orbiting debris blasted out in all directions, obliterating every single one of the leechers.

She surveyed the carnage, appearing satisfied–though taking no pleasure in it. She had merely done what needed to be done.

She turned to Daniel. "I'm Ionica Lux," she said simply. "Care for a ride?"

27

THE TRUTH SEEKERS

Daniel tried processing what had just happened, but who was he kidding? "You're a Truth Seeker . . . ?"

"Yes," she said.

"You're a girl."

Ionica narrowed her eyes, clearly puzzled by what that had to do with anything. "That too . . ." she said.

"How did you find us? The distress signal . . ."

"Was disabled. We know."

"The captain ordered no survivors."

"Pleasant fellow," she said, the confidence in her voice both infectious and unnerving. "We've been tracking the *WaKeenee* for weeks. What I don't know, Daniel Coldstar, is how you got on board this vessel. You're not listed in the ship's crew."

"I never told you my name."

The Truth Seeker appeared genuinely puzzled. "You're wearing an Identifier."

"A what?"

"You're broadcasting your identity to anyone within range. Pets or property are usually the only things that have them. And since you don't have any fur, I'm assuming you're the latter."

Daniel pulled back the torn remnants of his dugs at the chest, exposing the silver relic he was wearing. "You mean this?" he said. Though not identical, there could be no denying that it belonged to the same family as the one that she wore.

It was obvious she had not been expecting that. "No," she said warily. "Not that. Slaves don't have Aegi. How did you get that?"

Daniel really didn't like her reaction. He took a step back. "I found it," he explained.

"Where?"

"In the mines," he said.

"What mines?"

"Do you know about them?" he asked, hope in his voice.

"No . . ." she said. "Now hand it over before you get yourself hurt."

Wow, this girl . . . "No," he said, firmly.

"I'm not messing around. Only Truth Seekers bear the Aegis–"

Daniel whipped up a vortex shield so fast, Ionica barely had time to react. "What you see is what you get, I guess," he quipped. "Besides, it doesn't come off! I tried."

Ionica held her hands up, slowly. "Don't make any sudden moves. An Aegis in the wrong hands could cause a catastrophe. You obviously don't know what you're dealing with. For Fuse's sake, don't use it." She screwed up her eyes. "I mean, don't use it–more."

A noise, hardly noticeable to most people, but intimately familiar to Daniel–clicks from what once had been a functioning anatom voice box. So much had happened he'd forgotten about–

"Hex."

Daniel rushed over to the little anatom lying in pieces on the deck amid the wreckage. His legs were long gone; his matted fur had been ripped open at the chest, exposing a ghostly white biomass of tendrils extending out from a soft, egg-shaped body. The tendrils fused with interfaces throughout what was obviously a mechanical rat suit.

Daniel cradled him in his arms. "We have to help him."

"That thing's an antique. Good luck getting the parts," she said. "Besides, it's lost most of its fluid."

"He saved my life," said Daniel. "Besides, wise and all-powerful girl, can't you fix him?"

Ionica sighed. "I don't have time to argue. Pick it up; let's get it to the ship."

Marching back toward the hangar doors she had just

flown in through, she opened a communications channel. "The flight deck is secure," she said. "What about Darius Hun?"

"He didn't get far," someone replied. "We have him."

A few paces away a set of doors rolled open and a team of adult Truth Seekers escorted out a man in chains. The man who had brought the leechers on board. He appeared unnaturally calm about the whole turn of events, almost as though he had been expecting it.

An elder Truth Seeker, tall with powerful broad shoulders and a device under his nose that gave off vapors to help him breathe, stepped right up to him. "Darius Hun," he announced, in a commanding voice. "I've waited a long time for this."

"You mistake me for someone else," the prisoner replied calmly. "I am but a simple merchant."

The Truth Seeker ran the palm of his hand through the air, a holographic display panel appearing in its wake. Everything anyone would ever want to know about Darius Hun and his list of crimes scrolled through the air, while a holographic image of his face settled over the prisoner's own, confirming that he was indeed the wanted criminal.

"By the authority of the Guild of Truth, under Article Fifteen of the Sovereign Rights in Open Space Accords, I, Truth Guardian Raze Alioth, hereby place you under arrest. Where is the captain of this vessel?"

"I'm afraid I don't know who you're talking about."

"We will find your co-conspirator."

"Ask yourself," said the prisoner, in a mocking tone, "would the great Darius Hun allow himself to be captured by children on a training exercise–mere apprentices of the mighty Guild of Truth?"

"Blimey, does he ever shut up?" one of the younger Truth Seekers scoffed, emerging from behind the others. His scruffy hair looked like it could do with a wash. His boots needed a polish and his armored kilt had seen better days.

"Mr. Quick, you will treat our guest with respect," Alioth admonished.

"Yes, sir," the younger Truth Seeker replied, skulking off. When he spotted Ionica, he came marching over far more confidently.

His accent sounded different from everybody else's. Rougher. As though he'd seen a thing or two around the galaxy. "Aren't you impressed it was my team that got him?" he said, leaning closer, all cocky. "I'm that good."

Ionica pulled back. "Wow . . . your breath stinks!"

He was about Daniel's size and age too–although, like Blink, his eyes didn't appear to have any pupils either. Someone else from the Burn Worlds? He cupped his hand over his mouth and nose, checking his breath.

"What's she talking about?"

"Ben Quick," Ionica said, walking away. "You know the only thing you're really good at?"

"What's that?"

"Annoying the snot out of me."

One of the other younger Truth Seekers rolled his eyes. "Oh, here we go."

Ben glanced over at Daniel carrying what remained of Hex. "You know your anatom's broken? You should get that fixed."

"Really?" said Daniel. "Looks fine to me."

Taken aback, Ben glanced over at Ionica, while thumbing at Daniel. "I like him."

At the end of the flight deck, a pale-blueish craft with burnt-orange markings and shaped a little like a starfish came in to land. The core of the ship was a sphere, with a donut-shaped engine wrapped around it, off which several long arms extended. The Truth Seekers called her the *Equinox*.

"Find our guest some secure accommodations," Alioth ordered as the ship's boarding ramp extended out to the *WaKeenee* deck.

The elder Truth Seekers guided their shackled prisoner onto the ship, but just as the younger ones moved to follow, Darius Hun, for one brief moment, turned his head, letting his gaze settle solely upon Daniel. Was that a smile tugging at his lips?

Hard to know; in the next instant the criminal was led away.

A shiver ran down Daniel's spine. He glanced around, but the other Truth Seekers hadn't seemed to have noticed what had just taken place.

As they headed for the boarding ramp, Daniel glanced up at the underside. The scarred splintership was well worn and blackened around its exhaust vents, although the tips of its arms gleamed with colorful patterns–black-and-white checkerboards or jagged red-and-white teeth.

Daniel quietly watched the Truth Seekers going about their business, still coming to terms with the fact that he had been welcomed on board like a human being and didn't have to go creeping around anymore.

Inside the Sphere, everything was not as it seemed from the outside. The entire inner surface of the *Equinox*'s nerve center appeared transparent in every direction, giving the most jaw-dropping view of space as it maneuvered out of the *WaKeenee* flight deck. This glass display screen also projected the data on every star, planet, and other vessels within a parsec, while a hoop of light known as the REPIS system, or Relative Position in Space, made constant revolutions, updating the navigational data.

That, however, was perhaps not the most disorienting thing about being inside the Sphere. Every time the ship adjusted its course, the immense donut-shaped engine bearing the extended arms of the vessel spun around the Sphere, revealing the insides of the ship, with corridors stretching off and other Truth Seekers going about their business. While the Sphere itself never moved, always staying true to the galactic ecliptic, the way an old-fashioned compass always pointed north.

In a flash of brilliant light, the *Equinox* pierced through into Inspinity.

"We're heading for the Council of the Verdicti on Toshka," Ionica explained. "Unless there's somewhere else you were trying to reach. If it's on our route, we can drop you off."

Daniel shrugged. "Nowhere," he said. "I don't know what's out here. I don't even know where here is."

"Well," Ionica replied thoughtfully, "tell me whereabouts you snuck on board that freighter and I can tell you how far you got."

Daniel didn't know why he found that question so funny–maybe because he was just so exhausted–but when he laughed, tears streamed down his cheeks. "I don't know that either," he said.

"Usually when someone escapes from slavery, they take note of where they were, just so they don't end up there again," Ionica replied, with more than a little sass.

Daniel gazed off into his memories. "I really have no idea," he said. "I don't know how I got here."

"I don't understand."

Daniel held his face in his hands, sensing a great weight being lifted from his shoulders. If she were to ask him, he wouldn't be able to verbalize his thoughts, but he felt safe around her. He had no memory of ever feeling safe before now.

"I escaped," Daniel explained with hesitation. "From a relic mine."

"What's a relic mine?"

"We were enslaved by people who called themselves the Overseers." Daniel's throat constricted. He'd tried so hard not to think about any of this stuff. "They were trying to find something . . . something ancient."

"You said we," Ionica prodded gently. "How many were there like you?"

Daniel shrugged. "Thousands."

"Thousands?!"

"I was one of the older ones. Most were younger than me. A lot younger." He found his mind drifting back to the Racks, and bunk after bunk of little kids. "That place . . . it's all we've ever known. Just before I escaped, I found out that the Overseers were really just soldiers commanded by, uh, what were they called?" He racked his brain until he forced a memory to the surface. "The, uh . . . the Sinja?"

The name meant nothing to Daniel, but the immediate disgust on Ionica's face told him everything. "The Sinja?" she said, aghast. "You're telling me that you were a slave of the Sinja?"

"You know them?" Daniel asked, hopeful. Maybe now he'd start getting some answers.

Ionica scoffed. "Know them?" she replied. "Everyone's heard of them, but few can say that they actually know them."

"I don't understand."

"They like to remain hidden. Anonymous. But they have a web that stretches from one end of the galaxy to the other. You can bet that if there's a war–they're the ones who started it. Where there's poverty–they're the ones who created it," she explained, a lump in her throat. "They lie and manipulate from the shadows. Where there are planets, there are Sinja, hidden in plain sight, infiltrating governments, amassing power, sowing chaos, all to satisfy their greed. They're the reason I chose to become a Truth Seeker. They're the reason Truth Seekers even exist."

She looked away quickly, obviously embarrassed by such a rush of emotion in front of someone she hardly knew.

"Here you go," Ben Quick announced upon his return, setting a glass jar down on the table between them. Floating in a syrupy liquid, the ghostly white biomass that was once a rat named Hex swam happily back and forth. "What's left of your anatom," he explained.

Ionica snatched the jar out of the way. "Sit down. Shut up. And listen to this," she said.

Puzzled, but in no position to argue. Ben took a seat next to them. "Whenever you're ready," he said.

Daniel took a moment to collect his thoughts. So much had happened, how could he possibly organize it all into a coherent story?

He took a breath.

And when he was ready–Daniel told them everything.

Hours later, they found him a place to rest. There were no cabins aboard the *Equinox*. It wasn't a ship designed for long stretches in deep space. Instead there were bunk compartments hidden away inside the bulkheads of the long arms that stretched out from the Sphere, the central command structure.

Ionica hit a button and the white compartment door rolled up to reveal a bed and various useful little amenities. "It's more comfortable than it looks," she said.

"It'll be fine," Daniel replied, thankful. "What happens now?"

"Just get some rest," Ben advised.

Daniel nodded, dutifully lying down to do just that, Hex in a jar tucked up under his arm. He waited for about two minutes, and then, when he was fairly certain that the two Truth Seekers had gone, he got straight back up again.

He held the jar up to his face, watching Hex swimming around. "Don't worry, buddy," he said. "We'll fix this."

HEX A. DECIMAL 2.0

Bizarre and strange-looking anatoms littered the *Equinox* Repair Bay.

Some were huge, lumbering creatures that towered over the room. Others sported fleshy armored plates. Another had eight arms and a string of eyes all around its head.

Elsewhere, creature suits sat ready, their mechanical chests hollow and open, waiting for the biological parts to finish growing in the glass jars next to them.

Setting Hex in a jar down on a workbench, Daniel began perusing the spare part bins for anything that might be suitable.

"You must be Daniel Coldstar. The Sinja who isn't a Sinja. The stowaway boy," said the disembodied voice of a girl from somewhere across the other side of the Repair Bay.

"Hello?"

"I thought so," she said. With goggles perched on her head, and carrying bits of machinery and bundles of lightwire, the girl emerged from behind a parts cabinet and stuck out her hand at Daniel. She attempted to smile, but it looked more like a sort of grimace. "I'm Astrid Always. Always Astrid. Always right."

"Always getting on my nerves," said Ben Quick, coming through the door.

The girl stuck her nose in the air. "Ben doesn't like me because he's not as smart as I am."

"I don't like you because you're annoying," said Ben.

"Ionica doesn't seem to like you either," Daniel observed, looking at Ben.

Astrid laughed so hard it verged on a cackle.

"That's different," Ben protested.

"I'm not judging," said Daniel. "You just seem to have a way with girls, is all I'm saying."

"Oh, you noticed that too," Astrid remarked. "Amazing skill, isn't it?"

Ben tried his best to ignore her, keeping his focus on Daniel. "Why aren't you resting? And why didn't you tell me you wanted to work on your anatom?"

How was he supposed to respond to that? Might as well just come straight out and say it. "I didn't think you'd let me," Daniel said.

"Let you?" Ben seemed genuinely baffled. "I don't get to

decide what you can and can't do. You do."

"Somehow that's hard to believe."

Ben shrugged. "Listen. I just thought you might want a hand."

"Okay."

"And I've got some brilliant ideas. Brilliant. I say we give it a horn," Ben said. "I think it'd be spectacular, an anatom with a horn."

"What's a rat going to do with a horn?" Daniel asked.

Ben shrugged. "I don't know. Gore things."

"No horns. No trunks. No flappy wings," Astrid said, plopping herself down at a bench, setting to work on her own repair job, which was difficult to discern since she was only working on its internal skeleton. "If your anatom is as old as I've heard, it's been a rat for over a hundred years. It won't know how to be anything else," she said. "At the very least it should remain a quadruped. It won't know what to do with any extra limbs. Besides, you really shouldn't be trying to build an anatom without a blueprint anyway," she mused.

"I have schematics," Ben grumbled. "Here." He tossed a small glass card onto the table. Holocules fizzed into the air, forming a huge bearlike creature with metal pincers at the end of one arm–and a gigantic curved metallic horn.

Daniel couldn't quite fathom what he was seeing. Reading the description didn't help. "What's a catawampus?"

"Well, it's a, you know. A thing."

"Are they dangerous?"

Ben smirked, before realizing that Daniel was being perfectly serious.

"You've never seen a catawampus before?"

"No . . ."

"Oh, they're ferocious creatures," he explained, watching the miniature holocule anatom lumber around the workbench trying to smash anything in its path. "If they take a dislike to you–well . . ."

Inside the jar, Hex began swimming around, frantically trying to get Daniel's attention.

Daniel tried his best to decode all the tentacle waving. "He seems excited," he said, unconvinced. "But I'm not sure it's such a good idea."

"Well, if you're scared . . ."

Astrid rolled her eyes. "Stop it, Ben. He obviously doesn't know!"

"Know what?"

Ben brushed it aside. "Don't worry about it."

"There is no such thing as a catawampus," said Astrid, giving the design the most cursory glance. "And there's no such thing as this creature either. He just threw a bunch of bits and pieces together. You may as well call it Mish-Mash."

"It's called a catawampus," Ben insisted, annoyed.

"It's called a complete disaster," said Astrid, directing her focus back toward her own project. "Just saying."

Daniel turned on Ben. "You were making fun of me."

Ben shrugged. "Yeah."

"Huh," said Daniel, eyeing him closely. "Interesting."

"What's that supposed to mean?"

Daniel brushed it aside. "Don't worry about it–"

"Did you bring the corposum?" asked Astrid, setting a pair of magnifying goggles on her nose and peering over the rims at Daniel. "The squishy bit."

"Oh, right." Daniel set the jar down on the workbench, with Hex now happily swimming around inside it.

"Well, that's a start, I suppose," she said.

Over the next several hours Daniel and Ben gathered the parts they needed, or as close as they could get. But after a while, Astrid became so irritated watching the pair make so many basic mistakes, the boys had managed to rope her into the project too.

Only once she had tested all the circuits and could be absolutely certain that they wouldn't have to strip the thing down and start again did she tell Daniel that he could open up the jar and take Hex out.

"Now you can be pretty rough with him," she explained. "You have to press every inch of the corposum into that receptacle or he won't take–that's it. Good."

Daniel watched, enthralled, as Hex settled into his new creature suit, wriggling around and getting comfortable. Within a few minutes his tendrils extended out in all directions, attaching themselves to the suit, fusing with the all the necessary interfaces, until quite suddenly the anatom was taking his first baby steps.

Daniel punched the air. "All right, Hex! You're back!"

Hex wobbled on his feet, lashing out with his massive metal pincer to steady himself and chopping the workbench table in two. Utterly perplexed, the anatom didn't know which way to turn. He opened his mouth, but his lips flapped up and down without making any noise.

He glanced down at his paws. But they weren't paws. It was clear he recognized absolutely nothing about his own body. Petrified, he glanced around the workshop, wide-eyed.

"Hex, Hex!" Daniel urged. "It's okay, easy!"

But the anatom wasn't listening. Spying a tiny little hiding spot that would have served him well when he used to be a rat, he raced at it, only to smash into the wall.

"Hex! Slow down! Shhh!" Daniel beckoned Ben and Astrid over. "I think his voice box has a loose connection."

Astrid grabbed one of her tools, dashed over, and waved it in front of his eyes. In a calm, soothing tone, she said, "I just need you to open wide."

Hex glanced around. He understood. Nervously he opened his huge, gaping, bearlike maw and let the girl poke around inside–

The clicks and growls of spastic Mendese spewed out. "What have you done to me?" Hex cried. "My kids won't recognize me!"

It wasn't what Daniel had been expecting to hear. "You have kids?"

"Yes, of course!"

"How many?"

"Three hundred!"

"Three hundred kids?"

Hex smoothed down his fur indignantly. "I am one hundred and sixty-seven years old, and a rat. We like to breed."

"Erm, yes, not really a rat anymore. Sorry."

Hex smashed around, trying to find a mirror, completely unaccustomed to dealing with such a bulky size. "What am I?" he demanded. "What am I?"

"No idea, just a bunch of pieces we found and threw together."

Ben kept his distance. "That's a pretty good skill, being able to speak Mendese," he said. "How's he taking it?"

"Not well," Daniel said.

29

THE TRIAL OF DARIUS HUN

The skies over Toshka were filled with a huge array of Riggers, Junkadoos, and the really big core freighters that were too big to even consider a landing. The *Equinox* smoothly cut in between them, descending through the clouds toward a vast gray city, which had grown like a fungus out of the shells of previous vast gray cities.

Hovering above its assigned landing port, part of a complex of ports on the edge of a bustling market district, the long arms of the *Equinox* folded up over the Sphere, while its bulky landing gear extended out from underneath.

Daniel and Hex watched intently as a squad of senior Truth Seekers escorted Darius Hun from his holding cell to the planet's surface. Outside the port complex, a massive crowd had gathered, though it wasn't altogether clear whose side they were on.

In his familiar series of Mendese clicks, Hex said, "I think I'll wait by the ship."

"Darius Hun, your deception has been revealed. Your true identity exposed. You stand before this council to answer for your crimes, both numerous and egregious. Two hundred and sixteen charges, spanning thirty-one separate worlds."

The Council of the Verdicti, like the many similar councils throughout the galaxy, consisted of nine senior Truth Seekers. The proceedings took place under a security dome, which allowed an audience to watch the events anywhere in the galaxy, while leaving the chamber isolated and unencumbered by distraction.

Darius Hun stood in the very middle of the chamber, confined inside an energy field, while the nine Verdicti, their armor bloodred in color, encircled him.

Daniel sat transfixed, though in truth he understood very little about how the court worked. How could he? The Overseers had been anything but moral, or just. What he did know for certain was that the Truth Seekers who had captured Hun were not allowed to take part. As Ionica and Ben had explained, justice required those leading the trial to be "impartial," whatever that meant. So twenty-seven Truth Seekers had been selected at random throughout the nearest star systems. Nine of them looked at all the evidence and charges leveled against Hun and defended him from them. Nine other Truth Seekers looked at the same evidence and prosecuted Hun. The last nine were assigned to the Council of the Verdicti, and it was their judgment, based on listening to the arguments, that would decide Hun's fate.

It sounded impressive, but watching it unfold was a completely different experience. The entire trial had been a series of procedures and counter procedures, both technical and in many cases baffling. Perhaps one day Daniel would learn enough to fully understand how this system of justice worked, but for now everyone seemed to accept that this was simply how things were done.

Hun's crimes stretched back many years. His actions on board the *WaKeenee* seemed fairly minor compared to the other things he had gotten up to. The circumstances of his capture were also odd; usually he had two or three escape plans, but not this time.

"It's almost like he wanted to get caught," Daniel remarked quietly to Ben and Ionica.

The two Truth Seekers remained silent, not giving any clue as to whether they agreed or disagreed with his theory.

The lead prosecuting Truth Seeker continued with his summation. "These indictments, in matters of larceny, bribery, and, ultimately, murder have been well documented. They constitute a willful pattern of destruction meted out upon the lives of thousands of innocent citizens, in multiple jurisdictions; his ultimate goal, personal gain at any cost.

Members of this council, you have been presented with the evidence. It is time to render a verdict."

At that moment, nine thin glass columns rose up out of the ground, encircling Darius Hun. For his part, the accused appeared singularly unmoved.

"You understand the charges brought against you?" one of the Verdicti asked.

"I do," Hun replied.

"And yet you still plead guilty?"

Darius Hun turned around to face his questioner. A brief smile tugged at his lips. "Very, very guilty, your honor."

Another Verdicti spoke up. "Do you have anything to add in your defense?"

"If it pleases the court," Hun mused. "I have much to say, if you're willing to indulge me."

"It is not an indulgence," the Verdicti replied. "This is your last opportunity to speak. It is imperative that you do so."

Darius Hun turned around slowly, savoring the thrill of knowing that billions were watching him throughout the galaxy, even if he couldn't see them. When he was sure he had everyone's attention, he said, "War is coming."

The Verdicti listened, but appeared unmoved.

"Something very ancient has become new again," Hun explained, relishing this moment. "It is coming! For each and every one of you, there will be no mercy unless you bow down and pledge yourself before the Sinja! The Guild of Truth? You will be the first to fall! For your truth is powerless!"

The Verdicti silenced the chamber, allowing only the visual image of Darius Hun ranting and raving, spittle flying from his mouth.

One by one the Verdicti stepped forward, placing their hands on the ends of the glass columns in front of them, turning them from clear to red.

When the ninth was lit, a single Verdicti spoke for them all. "Darius Hun," she said, "you have been found guilty. You are hereby exiled to Felonis for the rest of your natural days."

And with that, the Verdicti filed out of the security dome, leaving Darius Hun to his raving.

"Your honors!" Ionica politely called out when they entered the public viewing chambers. She scrambled down from her seat, leaving Daniel and Ben behind. "My name's Ionica Lux, and I petitioned for a private conference with the Verdicti. Have you had time to consider the petition?" she said, her small frame dwarfed by the great leaders towering over her.

The Verdicti, their clothing rapidly changing color from ceremonial red back to the steely gray worn by all other Truth Seekers, considered her question.

"We have," one of them said. "But how do you know the boy is not lying?"

"I don't," Ionica said. "But I think that he believes what he is telling me is true."

"He may well believe every word of it," the Chief Verdicti remarked. "Even Darius Hun believes he is just. But belief alone does not make something just or true."

"We're Truth Seekers," Ionica reminded them. "Isn't it our duty to determine that for ourselves?"

The Chief Verdicti sighed. "I have already instructed the Guild to conduct a cursory investigation into some of the claims. We shall call upon you both when we have made a determination."

"Thank you, your honors," she said.

When they had filed out, Daniel jumped out of his chair. "I don't understand, what are they questioning?"

"Daniel, this is huge," Ionica explained, trying to sound as though she knew how to be patient. "Right now, the Verdicti have to be one hundred percent certain that your story bears any truth."

"To heck with caution!" said Daniel. "I just need a bunch of you guys to come back with me and free my friends."

"Daniel, it's not that simple."

"Why isn't it that simple?" he snapped.

"How do we know you're not leading us into a trap?"

Daniel didn't even begin to understand that line of reasoning. Why would he want to do that? What made them even think that? And then the realization hit him in the gut.

When the conference began a little while later, standing at the center of the Chief Verdicti's office, Daniel just came right out and said what they were all thinking. "I'm not a Sinja," he said.

The Chief Verdicti leaned against her long desk. "Do you even know what a Sinja is?"

Daniel shrugged. "I know you're afraid of them."

The objections and disquiet around the room were tempered only by the Chief Verdicti's no-nonsense response. "Truth Seekers do not fear the Sinja. We fear only what can happen when they gain control of those who are easily led, like that fool Darius Hun," she said, folding her arms. "But that still does not answer my question."

"I don't know who they are, only that I met one."

"Describe him to me."

Daniel cast his mind back, trying to separate what he had felt from what he had seen. He could find only one way to describe the mask that the Sinja wore. "He wore a face of blades."

Daniel glanced at the uneasy faces around the room. The Chief Verdicti rapped her fingers on the desk to what everybody else already knew. "Vega Virrus. Interesting."

One of the Chief's fellow Verdicti could remain silent no longer. "If Virrus is involved, then this is a plot that extends all the way up to–"

"Let us not allow the Lord of Lies," said the Chief Verdicti, "to further darken our discussion."

But the deed had already been done. The mere mention of such dark and powerful forces had an unsettling effect on everyone in the room.

Yet for Daniel, questions remained. Who was this Lord of Lies?

The Chief Verdicti looked down her pointed nose at Daniel, her voice grave. "The Sinja," she explained, "are the greatest threat to peace in the galaxy. They are liars and they are assassins. They like nothing more than to profit from chaos, misery, and war. They will turn friends against one another, they will persuade families to destroy one another, if it gives them what they want. Their greed is boundless."

"Why don't you just arrest them? Or destroy them?" said Daniel.

"We do, when we can find them. But because their true identities and the extent of their reach are unknown, and because they stay hidden in plain view, pretending to be part of the fabric of our society, it is not so simple. Any one of us in this room could be a Sinja, and on the surface, we would never know it."

"To that end," one of the other Verdicti interjected, "the Guild of Truth's preliminary investigation is complete. We can find no evidence of an increase in the number of missing children."

Daniel refused to believe what he was being told. "Where did you look, under your robes?"

Ben Quick laughed, and had to turn it into a cough to try to cover up his improper response.

The Verdicti explained, "It is possible that something has occurred on worlds where we have no jurisdiction, but I cannot answer to information that is unavailable."

"Besides," another Verdicti protested, addressing his comments to the Chief Verdicti directly, "without knowledge of this boy's origin, there aren't enough resources in the galaxy to conduct a thorough investigation. Where would we even begin?"

Daniel threw up his hands. "I can't believe this! You're not even going to try?"

Ionica rushed to block him from storming out. "Daniel, nobody said we weren't going to help. We're just identifying what the problems are. This is our way."

"Meanwhile thousands of grubs–just like me–are trapped, underground, starving, being forced to work and suffer every. Single. Day." Daniel turned on the Verdicti. "It's a miracle I made it out. And you're worried about evidence and where to begin? Begin with me, I'm standing right here! If you had evidence before I came in, you would have found us years ago! Of course you don't have any other evidence–they don't want us to be found."

Ionica laid a hand gently on Daniel's shoulder. "Please, show some respect–"

Daniel shook her off, the rage and frustration he'd been feeling for so long now far out of his control. "Respect? What about respecting me? If I were lying, would I be wearing this?" He ripped his dugs open to show them all the Aegis stuck to his chest. "This power has attached itself to me. It's freed me from a life of chains. If you don't believe me, put me on trial! I don't even know who I am. I have no memory of anything before the mines. Maybe someone watching will recognize me and come forward and answer your questions. Put all your great and learned minds at ease. I don't care if you think I'm speaking the truth or not. As the one who escaped, I have a responsibility. Help us. Please!"

How long had tears been running down his face? He could feel them dripping from his chin.

The Chief Verdicti nodded, thoughtfully. "I agree," she said.

Daniel's legs shook. He hadn't been expecting that. "Which part?"

"Though a public inquest of some description is appealing," one of the other Verdicti mused, "if he is telling the truth, we can't afford to let the galaxy see him just yet."

"Agreed."

Daniel didn't understand. If someone out there had answers, couldn't that only help? "Why not?" he asked.

"Then the Sinja would know that we know what they've been up to," Ionica explained, her voice soft but serious. "They'd shut down operations and move your friends before we even knew where to begin to look."

The revelation felt like a kick in the gut. "I hadn't thought of that," Daniel admitted.

"That's why I'm ordering you to take him to the Seven Summits," the Chief Verdicti explained to Ben and Ionica. "He will be safe there. The Fortress of Truth will provide shelter and assist all three of you in your investigation in any way that it can. If he wishes, he can train with the other students and learn the Way of Truth. Certainly he is going to need guidance on how to handle his Aegis. But from this moment on, Ionica Lux and Benjamin Quick, you are his guardians, and his actions are your responsibility."

Ben, who had had nothing to add to any of the deliberations, and who had been nodding off, nearly fell out of his chair. "Do what?"

"Your honor," Ionica protested, "we're Beacons ourselves, we're not even close to becoming full Truth Seekers yet."

The Chief Verdicti smiled. "Then this is going to be a challenge, isn't it?" she said. "Or are you not the same students who just aided the Guild of Truth in convicting one of the most wanted criminals in the galaxy?"

30

FORTRESS OF TRUTH

The splintership Equinox *flew* low over the rugged mountains of Orpheus Core, in final approach to the Fortress of Truth.

The Fortress, the lone building on the face of the planet, sat nestled within a ring of seven mountain peaks–the Seven Summits, though as far as Daniel could tell, it was more like six mountains and a stump.

All seven of the mountains, hollowed out and glittering with windows, were connected to the Fortress via bridges, except for the seventh, the stump, an exiled blackened pile of rubble that appeared to have been destroyed long, long ago.

It wasn't exactly a welcome party when Daniel, Hex, Ionica, and Ben stepped out of the hangar, but the bustling crowd of students going to and from classes certainly knew

Daniel had arrived and gave him long, sideways glances, if they didn't outright stare.

They didn't trust him.

Daniel glanced up at Hex, trying to steady him. "You okay?"

"I'm been complaining since you put me in this horrendous, drotefest of a suit! Haven't you been listening?"

Daniel tried his best to sound innocent. "I hadn't noticed," he said, shrugging. "Hey, wait up!"

Leaving the anatom to follow in his wake, he caught up with Ionica and Ben. This place was not what he'd been expecting. Like the mines, the students here were his age and younger, originating from more worlds than he could count.

"You live here?"

"Sometimes. When we're in training, or we're not assigned to an outpost," Ionica explained.

"Or when they give us a few days off and send us, er . . . home." Ben shuddered, as though that were the worst possible thing he could think of.

A short kid blocked their path, making a kind of grunting sound at Daniel, who couldn't tell if he was supposed to be impressed or if the kid was mocking him. Then he opened his mouth.

"I don't speak Chaff," Daniel said, trying to cut past him.

The kid stepped in his way again.

Daniel glanced around, trying to see a way through, but

it was obvious the boy wasn't going to move. "You're making a mistake," Daniel said quietly.

The boy put his hand on Daniel's chest. Daniel smacked it away.

"Touch me again and I'll stick your hand somewhere you really don't want it."

The kid had a look of utter shock on his face and, turning his back on Daniel, ran into the crowd and disappeared.

Ionica grimaced. "He was, er, welcoming you," she explained.

"Not everyone in the universe is a dootbag," Ben explained.

Embarrassed, Daniel slapped a hand over his mouth. "Oh . . ." He looked for the kid in the crowd. "I'm sorry!" he cried, but the kid was long gone.

Behind him, Hex started laughing, which in his new body sounded like a T-Dozer rolling in to level the place.

Daniel glowered. "You know, I can put you back in the jar."

Like the spokes on an ancient wheel, to reach any of the Seven Summits, the students first had to pass through the Fortress of Truth. In the center of the domed atrium stood an eight-legged fossil, a skeleton of an Arachnivore in an attack pose fighting a pack of Fathacond. The sign explained that it was just a baby, but it was the most complete example ever found. Arachnivores had been found on eighteen different planets before dying out some 250 million years ago at what exopaleontologists called the GEB–the

Galactic Extinction Boundary, when every intelligent alien race across the galaxy was wiped out in a single event.

Ionica shook her head. "Long before humans ever left home to journey on the Great Migration," she said, "whole worlds lived and died, leaving behind incredible legacies. Can you imagine what it was like to have known them?"

Daniel had a pretty good idea. Having worked the Sinja mines, and seeing what he had seen: all those machines of war.

Under his feet, the floor had shifted from stone to glass, exposing a vast hall of knowledge. A library of sorts, rows of digital information running between relics sitting encased under security domes. Inside one, a Truth Seeker stood in front of a large book lying on a podium, plucking stars and planets out of thin air and examining them like tree blossoms.

"What's she doing?" he asked.

"Studying," Ben explained hastily, "the Book of Planets."

"Star charts?"

"Not exactly," Ionica said. "Every planet in the entire galaxy is linked to that one book."

"Linked?" said Daniel. "How?"

"It's complicated," she said.

"And dangerous," Ben added. "Never go in there alone. You can get killed."

"From a book?"

Daniel watched the Seeker's companion, outside the

chamber, monitoring her progress carefully on a holocule console.

"Hmm," Ionica remarked, "I don't see the Keeper anywhere."

"Probably ripping another relic apart," said Ben. "One day he's going to get himself disintegrated."

"Well, let's just get Daniel to your room and get him settled," Ionica said, marching on ahead.

Ben pulled up short. "Wait a minute. My room?"

Ionica rolled her eyes. "Where else is he going to go?"

"Er, what about you?"

"He can't stay with me."

"Why not?"

"I'm a girl. And he can't stay with any of the other Seekers. They don't know him like we do."

"We just met him!"

"Quit shouting!"

"I am not shouting!" Ben's voice echoed throughout the Fortress of Truth.

Daniel eased off into the crowd. "Don't tire yourself out. I can find somewhere to bed down on my own."

"Oi, don't be daft," Ben called after him. "Of course you're staying with me."

"But I thought–"

Ben took a deep breath, trying to keep his cool. "I've just got two rules. Snore, and you're out on your ear."

"And the other?"

"For the love of the Fuse, take a bath. Or a shower. Or throw yourself into the Rogue River for all I care. Either way, scrub up. Then take whatever those sorry rags are that you're wearing and throw them away–better yet, burn 'em."

That all would have seemed reasonable to Daniel if the request had come from somebody else, but this Ben Quick kid, with his matted hair and his muddy boots?

"Have you looked in a mirror recently?"

Ionica laughed at that.

31

ZUBENEL GENUBI'S GALACTIC HISTORY OF THE EXODUSSIC AGE

"Catch!" said Ben, tossing over one of those armored Truth Seeker kilts. "They're called sleeks. They should fit you."

Up close, Daniel realized he'd never seen a fabric quite like it, if you could call it a fabric. The entire thing seemed to be made up of tiny hexagonal pieces of metal; cold to the touch on the outside, surprisingly warm and soft on the inside. "Should I be wearing these? People might think I'm a Truth Seeker."

"I'm pretty sure they won't," Ben replied, almost too confidently.

Ben's room, now also Daniel's room, was situated high up in the Second Summit, with a view looking out at the wilderness of Orpheus Core, rather than inward at the Fortress of Truth.

For the longest time, Daniel just sat on the edge of his new bed, clutching his sleeks, watching the clouds drift by.

Ben, on the other hand, couldn't see the appeal. "Are you going to shower or what? Classes start in ten minutes."

Reluctantly, Daniel did as he was told. Although the first problem was trying to figure out how to take his smelly old mining dugs off when the Aegis on his chest refused to budge. He clawed his fingers under the fastenings down the front and managed to yank some of the fabric out from underneath it, but he had to keep his fingers there while he tugged the rest out with his other hand.

When he was done, the Aegis pressed harder against his bare chest.

Great. He was going to have to shower still wearing this thing. He would have to keep reminding himself that this was all perfectly normal and that he wasn't under attack, or he'd end up accidentally destroying the entire bathroom.

It took a while to figure out all the controls; there was water and sonic waves, and try as he might he couldn't get the autodry to work, so he used a towel. He didn't think he'd ever been this clean in his life. He wasn't sure if he liked it, but he'd go with it for now.

When it was time to put on the sleeks Ben had given him, that was a whole other issue. There didn't appear to be any fastenings. How did anyone put these things on? Maybe it stretched. He found the opening to the kilt section and decided to try pulling it on over his head.

That was when things took an unexpected turn. The tiny metallic hexagons that made up the garment began breaking apart. At first, Daniel thought that maybe he'd ripped it, but then the individual pieces began moving–all on their own! They raced down his body, forming sleeves, and a kilt, wrapping around his chest and back, reconfiguring into the perfect size.

Once they had settled into their final shape, Daniel glanced down, mesmerized, as the tiny hexagons pulled back from the Aegis, before burrowing under it and lifting it up onto its finished surface.

Ben gave a modest nod of approval when Daniel took a step. "Not bad. You actually *do* look like one of us, huh," he said, handing him a pair of boots. "Come on."

Daniel wasn't sure what to expect when they arrived at the lecture hall. Nothing about the whole process seemed familiar at all. The room was circular, with benches ringing an open area in the center. The benches themselves rose progressively higher so that the Truth Seekers taking the class looked down on Zubenel Genubi, the instructor.

Genubi had a narrow face and long limbs, and when he spoke his voice sounded like air being squeezed out of a balloon.

"Can anyone tell me," he asked, "the name of the planet where humans originated?"

The first Truth Seeker to try to answer the question said, "Dirt."

Another one said, "Clay."

It turned out the name of the planet was Earth.

The class didn't go any faster from there. Genubi plodded through the timeline of how humans left this planet Earth in the Great Migration some ten thousand years ago because there wasn't enough food and water to go around. Humans depended on other worlds to survive.

Genubi also talked about how humans were not united when they left Earth. They were separated by what were called countries, and also by languages, and these separations were what led to the nature of humankind throughout the galaxy today.

After two hours of this, Daniel had progressed from being mildly bored to being frustrated and angry.

What was the point in having someone stand there and tell you all this stuff when you could just get plugged in and load it all into your head in a matter of seconds? It seemed like such a waste of valuable time.

This is what the Verdicti on Toshka had wanted for him? It felt like a pointless distraction.

When a brief alarm echoed throughout the chamber for recess, Daniel was instantly on his feet.

"Why am I here?" he asked. "Why am I learning things I'm never going to use?"

Ben wasn't sure he understood. "It's a history class," he said.

"What is the point of it?" Daniel demanded, "For me. What is the point? How does it help me find where I came from? How does it help me get back there?"

"It doesn't. We learn the histories of worlds so we don't make the same mistakes all over again."

"Oh, don't worry, we're not repeating old mistakes," said Daniel. "We're making whole new ones. I can't sit around while my friends are in chains. I need to be out there doing something about it!"

32

SKYRIDER'S GORGE

Daniel ran.

Out of that class. Out of that fortress. He just had to get away. Far away. Out across the open grassland and the loosely wooded foothills where the abandoned columns and fallen arches of the once-mighty bridge to the Seventh Summit stood like petrified giants. Scrambling through the thicket until he emerged onto a bluff overlooking Rogue River and the Seventh Summit beyond, his aching lungs filled with the fresh scent of tree sap and fallen leaves.

He stood, his sides aching, watching Orpheus Core's lone, piercing blue sun, turning violet as it set, slipping behind the charred ruin to reveal a sea of unfamiliar stars in the twilight sky.

It wasn't enough. He needed more than just being able to breathe.

In a bright burst of Aegis energy–

Whompff!

He bounded over the swirling waters, landing at the foot of the Seventh Summit. Where once an impressive Truth Seeker stronghold had been carved into the heart of the mountain now stood the remnants from its total destruction.

The ruins were black with soot and damp from having been abandoned for so long. Bizarre creeping vines and other strange-looking plants had taken root along the walls. The flapping wings of a startled creature fluttered somewhere up near an open window.

Something about this place seemed familiar somehow. Though he wasn't sure why. Perhaps it just reminded him of the mines.

The peak of the summit was long gone, exposing swathes of rooms to the elements. As Daniel made his way inside, negotiating the crumbling corpse of a staircase, he couldn't shake the eerie feeling that the spirits of the dead were watching him. Everywhere he looked, charred beds sat tucked inside burnt-out rooms, reminders that children had slept here, before the evil came.

And there it was, that rage in his belly that he thought he'd gotten a handle on.

Here he'd been trying to make them understand that there were a thousand lost kids out there somewhere dying under Sinja rule–not hypothetically, but actually.

Why were they being so slow to help? Were they afraid?

Daniel pushed on through the ruins, trying to find a way out, but the farther he went, the worse it got, until finally he ran into a dead end.

Why did it feel like he was back in the mines?

In that moment, all the frustration he'd been dealing with came bubbling up from deep within, reaching directly into his Aegis.

Wwwwwwhhhhooooommmmpffffffff!

The blast radiating from his Aegis was so powerful, it blew out the walls in every direction, the dead end opening up to the outside once more, revealing a massive blackened fissure running down the back side of the Seventh Summit, as though some powerful ancient force had torn the mountain open like an animal looking for bugs.

"Feel better?"

The voice was Ben's.

"How long have you been standing there?"

"Long enough," Ben said, joining him at the edge of the precipice to see the view for himself. "Skyrider's Gorge. We use it for training. You should try racing Ionica down here sometime. She'll kick your butt."

"The Sinja did this, didn't they?" said Daniel.

"A very long time ago. Way before I was born."

"Is this why you're all so afraid of them?"

"Afraid of the Sinja?" Ben sounded amused. "Bloody right we're afraid of them. But not for the reasons you think."

"Enlighten me."

"We don't care what they do to us," Ben explained. "It's what they do to others that frightens us. How they can twist minds, make brothers fight brothers, make sisters murder sisters. There are entire systems out there," he added, "whole worlds controlled by the Sinja, where the people do exactly the opposite of what's good for them, because they believe the lies so completely that they can't see the truth, even when it's presented to them. Slavery is freedom. Up is down. Black is white. Good is evil."

"Then why are the Verdicti giving up on them?"

"Who said anything about giving up?" said Ben.

33
ALLEGIANCES

The entrance to the Vault sat buried deep in the heart of the mountain, where the feet of the Seven Summits became one. Words could not adequately describe what lay before Daniel when he stepped through its gleaming tritanium arch. Truth Seekers, students and teachers alike, came and went lost in conversation. Behind them, a honeycomb of gigantic tritanium buttresses crisscrossed throughout the immense space, creating distinct areas of learning. One entire section held genuine ancient paper books on shelves; some of them had to be thousands of years old and were being treated with reverence by the Truth Seekers handling them. Another section seemed more like an arboretum of knowledge: data storage columns towered like trees, and holocule images of the digital documents they contained projected out like branches and blossoms for the Truth Seekers to leaf through.

And at the center of it all, a collection of ancient artifacts was displayed upon a circle of gleaming pedestals, each one a reflection of the lost civilizations that had created it.

Daniel's pulse quickened as he read the inscriptions:

The Anthydion Device. Discovered EE 8923 by Indigo Cort. Planet: Mandaradan. Civilization: Unknown.

Starflake Extractor. Discovered EE 7790 by Suko Reen. Planet: Tantara. Civilization: Destronomer.

The scorched relic looked a little like a crab that had been heat-blasted almost to the point of disintegration; deep cracks ran throughout its armor, a patchwork of discolored plating that bore the faint trace of rainbows. "What's a starflake?" Daniel asked.

"You're wearing one right now," Ionica replied, emerging from behind a line of silent data columns. "No two starflakes are alike, which is why every Aegis is different," she said. "I didn't think you'd come."

"I nearly didn't," Daniel admitted, glancing down at the geometric relic on his chest. "Where can you find starflakes?"

"In the solid core of a dying star," she said.

No wonder the Extractor looked the way it did. Daniel looked her in the eye. "Ben said you had a plan."

"Not my plan. Our plan."

From behind another column, Ben stepped into the open alongside Astrid Always, the girl who had helped him rebuild Hex.

"Ben tells me you want to take on the Sinja, all by yourself," she said, "without any idea what you're doing?"

Daniel didn't know what to be more surprised by: that they were here too, or that Ben seemed to have told just about everybody. "I was thinking about it," he said.

"That's the stupidest thing I've ever heard."

"Thanks."

"Do you know how many Truth Seekers died trying to secure these relics to make sure they didn't fall into the hands of the Sinja?"

Daniel shook his head.

"A hundred and three. A hundred and three of the bravest, most highly trained Truth Seekers ever to come out of the Fortress of Truth." The sheer anger in her voice alarmed even Astrid. She clenched her teeth. "And you think you can do better than them?"

Was that a tear in her eye? "I didn't know," he said quietly.

"There's a lot you don't know, Daniel," Ionica replied.

Daniel refused to be made to feel guilty. "You know what I do know?" he replied. "If I had the most dangerous artifacts in the galaxy, I wouldn't leave them lying around for just anyone to pick up." To prove his point, he reached out to snatch up the scorched artifact, only to find his hand plowing through it. A hologram.

"It's not really there," said Ben, rolling his eyes. "None of them are."

"The real artifacts," Astrid explained, "are kept in vaults throughout the galaxy. These are security images."

Ionica shook her head. "You want to battle the Sinja, people who lie with every breath, and you can't tell the difference between a hologram and a real relic?"

"You tricked me."

"Nobody tricked you, you just didn't look, because you don't know how. You have to question everything. That's the first rule. Don't believe what you see. Don't believe what you're told. Question authority, which you seem to be good at already. Learn *how* to think, not *what* to think. That's the way of the Truth Seeker!"

"But I'm not a Truth Seeker!" he roared defiantly.

"Or are you?" Ionica replied, raising an eyebrow.

"And maybe you need to realize you're not going to stop me from finding my friends."

Surprise danced in Ionica's eyes. "Don't you think we know that?"

The three of them gathered around. "We're not trying to stop you," said Ben. "Without guidance, without training, you'll end up dead, or worse."

Daniel couldn't imagine what might be worse than being dead.

"This galaxy is riddled with Sinja influence," he added. "Like a disease eating away at anything good. Heck, you lived under Sinja rule for how long and didn't even know it–"

"Well, he is twelve years old," interrupted Hex.

Daniel did a double take. "Where did you come from?"

"From over there."

Daniel glowered.

"I heard you ran away. Again. I went looking for you."

"What is he saying?" Ben chimed in.

"Nothing important."

Hex snorted dismissively. "Charming," he said.

Ben continued, "My point is, it's okay to admit a little defeat. It's how we learn. And you have a lot of things to relearn."

"We're your friends too," Astrid said. "You're not alone. We just want to do everything we can to help prepare you."

Daniel knew he had to accept their help.

Over the course of days and weeks, they showed him how to put the Vault to good use, how to search for information, and how to follow clues. Together they mapped out the most important things he needed to learn, such as Mastery of the Aegis. Every day he practiced a whole set of moves to expand his abilities, taking classes with a number of Truth Seekers whose abilities ranged from beginner to expert.

The History of Ancient Alien Cultures and Artifacts was probably the next most important class to take. The Sinja had been making Daniel mine for relics, after all. Daniel might be able to pick up clues as to what they were ultimately searching for. Philosophy of the Sinja struck them all as important too, as was Needle Drives and Star Lore.

Everything else could wait.

After a couple of weeks, Daniel started getting the hang of how to take classes, instead of just plugging in the data. He learned to ask questions of his teachers, participate with other students, and not be afraid that he didn't always know the answers. Understanding that he didn't know all the answers was the second rule, and following it had the most unexpected effect: he stopped being afraid. Before long he felt confident enough that he wanted to go further. Dig deeper. But his classes weren't giving him what he needed. And why should they? Daniel was the only person at the Fortress of Truth who knew what a relic mine was like. He alone had the best shot at finding it.

But how to find something that nobody knew how to find?

And so for a few hours each night, while his new friends slept, Daniel took himself and Hex back down to the Vault to conduct his own investigation into where he had come from and how he was going to get back there. He had the star charts of the *WaKeenee* still stuck in his head, so that was a help. The evidence records from the trial of Darius Hun were still accessible, along with data showing who owned the ship, what it carried, and where it had traveled.

Resolutely he examined every clue he could lay his hands on, even if at times it felt as though he was getting nowhere, but he refused to give up.

And then one night, quite by chance, when Daniel had gathered his belongings, he passed by the sparkling glass chamber that held the mysterious Book of Planets.

"What is this Book of Planets anyway?" Hex asked.

Daniel chose not to look up from what he was reading as he walked. "Some kind of star chart, best I can figure out."

"I don't get it. What's so special about that?"

"It's live," Daniel explained. "It updates in real time. You can hop from planet to planet like a god. Breathe their air."

Hex clicked excitedly. "Wow, I'm surprised you don't check it out."

"I can't."

"Why not? That sounds right up our alley!"

Hex had seemed uninterested in the Vault at first, but after a while Daniel had coaxed the anatom to keep him company. Now it had reached the point where he was more eager to keep going back than Daniel was.

"I don't know," Daniel said, with a sigh. He glanced up. "It could kill me."

"How so? And why all this me business? Don't you mean we? We could get killed. . . . If anyone is hopping around planets like a god, it is going to be me."

"You don't understand," he said, still trying to decide if it was worth the risk. "They said it takes great concentration.

Besides, I don't want to betray their trust."

"Betray their trust? Here you have access to something better than any star chart, a device that can let you peer into any planet in the galaxy, in real time, and they won't show you how to use it? Is there something they don't want you to know?" asked Hex. "Seems to me they're the ones betraying your trust."

"If I didn't put you back together with my own two hands, I'd think you were a Sinja with all this talk. Now be quiet. I'm trying to think."

A little while later, Daniel reluctantly got up and peered through the glass at the massive Book of Planets sitting on its podium in the middle of the chamber, its cover worn and fragile. He could only imagine what secrets were held within its pages; if only he knew how to access them.

"Kid," Hex said, "I bet you've seen more of this galaxy than they have, and survived drote knows what, and you're going to let them tell you what you can and can't do?"

"If you're so eager, you go in there and kill yourself."

"I'm an anatom, the door won't open for me."

"Come on," said Daniel. "It's late. Let's get some rest."

Distinctly disappointed in Daniel, Hex shook his head and slowly started making his way toward the exit.

Daniel pressed his nose against the cold glass. Maybe he could take just a quick peek?

Without warning, the door rolled open.

Stunned, Daniel glanced around. Someone had forgotten to lock the door. "Hello?" he called out.

Hex glanced back over his shoulder. "There's no one else here, kid. Just you and me. Go on. Step inside. It's practically an invitation."

Daniel hesitated. "This doesn't feel right, Hex. Every planet in the galaxy is supposed to be in here," he said. "What if we . . . break something?"

"Only one way to find out."

The Book of Planets was no ordinary book. It couldn't be read; it had to be experienced. Daniel didn't know what that meant, really, but he wanted to find out.

Whenever he had seen Truth Seekers at work, tiny planets and stars literally jumped from its pages and swirled around them. It seemed simple enough.

Hex was right–what could possibly be so dangerous about something as simple as a book?

The answers were right there in front of him. If he had the courage, all he had to do was look. Besides, who would know?

Daniel pushed the door open and stepped inside.

34

THE BOOK OF PLANETS

Daniel felt it immediately, a presence watching him.

There was great power here, as though the Book of Planets were alive.

Daniel approached the hefty tome carefully. Now he understood why it was kept inside the chamber. Not to protect the book, but to protect everyone else from the book.

Maybe he shouldn't be doing this. He turned to leave, pushing on the glass door–

It wouldn't move.

He thumbed the controls. Locked. Now how had that happened?

Flick. Flick.

Daniel started to panic. The hair on the back of his neck stood on end. And for the first time that Daniel could remember, Hex was speechless. Slowly, very slowly, he glanced over his shoulder.

Flick. Flick.

The Book of Planets had creaked open, its pages flipping one by one by some unseen hand.

"Very funny," said Daniel.

He quickly surveyed the room to see if he could spot anyone in the library. But deep down he already knew the answer. There was nobody else here.

The Book of Planets was alive.

Daniel marched back to the podium and grabbed the heavy book with both hands. He struggled to lift its covers. The pages refused to stop flipping back and forth, faster and faster, whipping the air into a storm, until a searing light blasted out from between them, knocking Daniel off his feet.

Daniel clutched at his aching chest, trying to catch his breath. He snatched his hand away almost immediately. He glanced down.

His Aegis stirred, doing something he'd never seen it do before–it glowed.

Above his head, comets, stars, and entire worlds tumbled from the pages of the Book of Planets, gliding into orbits around the chamber, forming entire star systems with multiple planets, orbiting single and sometimes multiple suns.

"All right . . ." said Daniel, getting to his feet. "If that's how you want to play it."

Daniel closed his eyes and the star charts of the *WaKeenee* came spilling out of his memory into the air above him, with the force of the Aegis matching up the alignments until what he saw in his mind's eye fit exactly with what he was being shown in this powerful book.

Where the ship's charts gave him names of systems, the Book of Planets gave him experiences—the sounds, the textures, the vibrations, the sense of being on those planets. All his memories, holes and all, fell into place and began to make some sense.

With each passing orbit, Daniel caught metallic elements on his tongue, or felt the faintest whiff of exotic scents drift into his nostrils. As the planets crisscrossed, he quickly discovered that he could trace them just by picking up their trails. It revealed a pattern at work in the galaxy that he would never have seen just by looking. He could sense which planets belonged together just by their chemical composition. He could sense which planets were foreign, and which were familiar. . . .

He turned his attention to that desolate region of space Hex had called the Embers, hunting for the smell of misery; that old reek of oil, and grease and disease—that rancid world of the Overseers.

There! Was that it . . . ?

It came again, disappearing as fast as he'd found it. He turned on his heel, desperately trying to find the source of the odor. So many planets, so many trails; which one was it?

Daniel closed his eyes, focusing on the memories, trying to capture a trace of them in the air.

It seemed like such an impossible task. Until . . . was that it? Had he found them?

Daniel snapped his eyes open, confronted with the awesome beauty of flying through an alien world, until–

A blistering sun shot past his face. Then another. And another. Five in all. Searing fireballs singeing his hair and face, leaving streaks of red, blistered skin in their wake.

Daniel cried out in agony.

He threw his hands up as more objects tumbled toward him, asteroids with the power of fists and gas giants filling the chamber with noxious fumes, snuffing out the oxygen, leaving him choking and dizzy.

Frantic, Daniel looked around. He couldn't see the Vault. He couldn't see the book. He was lost in an illusion!

He reached out. There had to be a way to get it to close! But the more he struggled with the book, the more the atmospheric pressure became so crushing that it literally began squeezing the life from his bones. And it was at this point that Daniel cried out, "I'm sorry!"

And then, quite suddenly, from the misty fumes, a warm hand reached out for him.

Daniel had no way of knowing whose hand it was. But as he took what felt like his last gasp of air, he reached out and grabbed it.

WAY OF THE TRUTH SEEKER

Daniel rolled onto his side, coughing violently, his throat burning.

"Here, drink this," the stranger commanded, forcing a cup of milky liquid into his hands. "Quickly, quickly."

It tasted bitter, but Daniel did as he was told, gulping it down until it was all gone.

It took a moment before the burning sensation began to ease. When he could breathe again, he thanked the man and handed the glass back, his hand shaking.

The stranger gazed down on Daniel with lively eyes; he had a restless nature that quickly drew him away. In constant motion, his kilt swishing every time he took a step, he darted around the strange room, filled with contraptions and elaborate instruments. Pieces of enginoids were stacked in one corner, and the anatomy of an anatom was displayed in the other. The stranger, always doing three things at once, never rested.

After quietly watching the stranger for a little while, Daniel asked, "How did I get here?"

From behind a pile of junk, the stranger said, "With my two bare hands I picked you up, threw you over my broad and impossibly strong shoulders, and carried you."

Daniel sat up. "You did what?"

The stranger poked his nose around the corner. "You don't believe me?"

"No."

The stranger appeared insulted. "Why not?"

"Because you're . . . short. I'm probably bigger than you."

The stranger narrowed his eyes, stepping out from behind his creations. Daniel stood perhaps a head taller, though the stranger was much wider. He clearly had the face of an adult, but his limbs were proportioned like a child. "Well done, Captain Obvious. Ionica was right about you. Remember her? The girl who saved your life."

The stranger kind of reminded him of Ogle Kog from back in the mines, but his physique appeared very different. "Did you grow up on a high-gravity planet?" Daniel asked.

The stranger appeared even more insulted. "No," he said, incredulous.

"Then why are you that shape?"

"I was born this way!"

"Who are you?" Daniel demanded.

The stranger's mind didn't pause, even for a moment. "Who am I?" he said. "Who are you?"

"I'm Daniel Coldstar, slave number forty-one eighty-two. But you already knew that."

The stranger glanced over at him with a twinkle in his eye. He didn't seem particularly old, but he had the presence of an old soul. He seemed to like Daniel's response. "Didn't anyone ever warn you about the Book of Planets, Daniel Coldstar?" he said. "You could have gotten yourself killed. Why didn't you use your Aegis for protection?"

Daniel glanced away. "I didn't think of it," he said quietly. "Besides, if somebody hadn't left the door open, I wouldn't be in this mess."

The stranger considered what Daniel had told him, but if his eyes were any indication, his mind was an endless cycle of supernovae. "There's nothing wrong with being curious," he replied thoughtfully. "I did the same thing when I was your age. But don't blame others for your irresponsibility."

"It's true. The door was open. How else could I get inside?"

"But nobody asked you to step inside, did they?"

"No . . ."

"You made that choice alone. The consequences are entirely yours," the stranger remarked.

Daniel thought about what he had said. "What are the consequences?"

"You tell me." The stranger stopped in his tracks. "You're the Truth Seeker now. What did you find?"

Daniel didn't know how to respond, or even if he should. The stranger held such a powerful, magnetic force of personality that Daniel felt compelled to say something–but what?

Standing behind one of the larger desks, the stranger snatched up a complex-looking monocle and pressed it to his eye. Peering down his nose, he set to stretching out schematics and perusing their contents, comparing an elaborate device on the table with the picture of a similar-looking object rotating next to it.

Daniel slowly got to his feet. "I have one request," he said.

"What's that?"

"Please don't tell anyone what happened. If the Keeper ever found out . . ."

The stranger glanced up from his studies, impatience saddled on his face like a feedbag on a Hammertail. "Have you ever met Tor Torin?"

"Who's he?"

"The Keeper. He does have a name, you know."

"Oh," said Daniel. "No."

"Then how do you know how he'd react?"

"I don't," Daniel admitted. "But I doubt he'd react well, no matter how wise he's supposed to be."

The stranger seemed troubled. "That's all you've been

told? No one ever mentioned how fantastic he is?"

"Fantastic?"

"He's an extraordinary man. It's common knowledge."

Whoever this man was, he was more than a little cracked, Daniel decided.

"No one ever told you how he fought the Beast of Amaranth?"

"No."

"Rescued the Krittika from Scalpernauts, single-handed?"

Daniel shook his head. "Sorry."

The stranger threw his monocle down in disgust and began mumbling to himself. "Youth! What's the point in having a reputation if nobody knows what it is?"

"Pardon?"

"Nothing."

"All I know," said Daniel, "is that this Torin person can kick me out of here on a whim, and I'm not about to let that happen just yet."

The stranger pressed the monocle back to his eye once again and resumed studying the device. "Why not?"

"I need to rescue my friends. That's why I searched the Book of Planets, for all the good it did me." Daniel stood at the edge of the desk, watching the stranger examine the mysterious object, taking careful note of every detail.

"What is that thing?" Daniel asked. "Did you build it?"

"Dear me, no. I didn't build this," replied the stranger, running his keen eye over the ornate surface, probing its imperfections with a tiny screwdriver. "But it does look like the picture, doesn't it? Fortunately, it doesn't appear to be working."

Daniel didn't understand why that was fortunate.

"It's a Thought Detonator," said the stranger, tapping the image on the schematic. "Nasty little thing. A relic from the War of Wills." He set the device back down on his desk. "I found this one being sold as a paperweight," he said. "Which raises some very serious questions. First, where did it come from? Second, who had enough knowledge of Thought Detonators to disarm it? And third, nobody's made paper in over two thousand years, so why would anybody need a paperweight?"

"Maybe somebody found it and they didn't know what it was? I don't know what one is," Daniel said simply.

Such brutal honesty took the stranger by surprise. "A Thought Detonator," he explained, gravely, "has only one purpose. To lie in wait for Truth Seekers–and destroy them."

Daniel hadn't even considered that a Truth Seeker could be killed. They all seemed so . . . invincible. "How?" he asked.

"By taking a Truth Seeker's greatest strength, and turning it against them," he replied. "I had hoped never to see their like again."

Taking the device in both hands, the stranger carefully set it high up on a far shelf. "There isn't a Truth Seeker alive who wouldn't instantly recognize the threat posed by the return of one of these insidious little nasties. We were meant to find this," he said. "As a warning."

It took a moment for the stranger's words to sink in before Daniel realized their importance. "A warning? From who?"

"Precisely," said the stranger, striding back to his desk and gathering up his tools. "Though I fear that by the time we find the answer to that question, it may be too late."

Daniel hadn't thought about it much before now, but in joining the Guild of Truth he had taken sides in a galaxy he knew very little about. "Do Truth Seekers have many enemies?" he asked.

"There will always be those who feel threatened by the truth," said the stranger, taking his bundle of ratchets and screwdrivers, and other odds and ends, over to a chest, pulling open the lid, and dumping them into it in no particular order. "Consider," he said. "Why might somebody lie to you?"

Daniel thought deeply on the question. "To hide something?"

The stranger nodded. "That's one reason. There are many others. Can you think of any more?"

"To make you think differently."

"About?"

"Anything. A person, a piece of information."

"I see. So why might somebody tell you the truth?"

"To reveal something."

"Ah, revealing something implies that there was a lie trying to hide it to begin with. What if there was no lie? What would the truth be then?"

Daniel was truly puzzled. "Makes you think about the subject more, I guess."

"Would you say then that it gives us focus?"

Daniel shrugged in agreement. "Sure."

"Aha!" the stranger said with a smile. "And when we focus, what do we see? We see possibilities. You see what we have discovered together? We have discovered the truth. And the truth is that lies have a purpose. They are designed to sway you. Distract you. Confine you. Limit you. But the truth? There is nothing freer than truth. No higher authority. The truth just is, but lies serve a master. And a master of lies craves power, and to remove his power is the greatest threat that he will ever know."

Now this was something Daniel understood. Deep inside himself, even when the Overseers had told him that the universe was a certain way, he knew there had to be something better. Even when the Sinja had told him if he stepped outside the mines he would surely die–he knew the truth lay elsewhere.

"You see!" said the stranger, pointing at him. "I see it in your eyes. You recognize this as truth, don't you?"

"I do," said Daniel. "I felt it. I knew it. Will I always be able to tell the difference between a lie and the truth?"

"Finding the truth is a lifelong journey and it is never an easy one. That is the Way of the Truth Seeker. Remember, the biggest mistake we can make is to stop asking questions; not only of others, but of ourselves."

"I don't understand."

"Sometimes, as humans, Daniel, we can lie to ourselves, and we often do." The stranger rounded the table and jabbed a finger at the dormant silver Aegis on Daniel's chest. "You have trouble removing your Aegis."

Daniel glanced down at the troublesome silver relic. "I've never been able to take it off."

"Where does it sit on your body?"

Now that was a strange question. "Uh, right here."

"But where, on your chest?"

It took a moment to realize what the stranger was getting at. "Over my heart," he said.

"All the Aegis asks from you," said the stranger, "is purity of intent. The Aegis knows your head and your heart. When they are in conflict, your Aegis will not function. You must control it both in mind and in spirit. You must know what you wish it to do, and you must believe that it will be done."

"You're saying that it can read my mind?" asked Daniel.

The stranger rolled his eyes in frustration. "You're not much of a poet, are you? Yes, okay, it can read your mind. The reason you can't remove it is because deep down you don't want to, and the Aegis knows that."

"Why would I not want to remove it?"

The stranger shrugged. "Because it protected you once and you hope it will do it again? Or you just think you look really great wearing it. I don't know. The Aegis reads minds. I don't."

Daniel glanced down at the ancient device in wonder. "How does it even do what it can do? Is it magic?"

The stranger almost choked. "Is it what?!"

"Magic?"

"Magic?" The mere mention of the word seemed to leave a bad taste in the stranger's mouth. "Of course it's not magic," he raved. "This is science!"

"Then how does it work?"

"Haven't the faintest idea." The stranger turned tail and went back to his contraptions. "Humans didn't make them. Some very ancient intelligence scattered them throughout the galaxy, and we Truth Seekers were able to utilize them."

"You must know something. All that power. It's incredible. Did you ever open one up to find out?"

The stranger sighed and leaned across his desk. "Yes, I did once. . . ."

"And?" Daniel asked eagerly.

"It was empty."

"What?"

The stranger shrugged. "The act of opening it made it empty. The nexus of what was inside vanished, escaped, disappeared. Poof! I know how it works in theory. Just not in practice."

Daniel pulled his arm back, creating a perfect whirling shield of air. "How? How does it do this?"

The grave expression on the stranger's face grew darker with every passing moment. "We call it the Fuse," he said. "Though it's had many names through the ages. The Source. The Core. At the beginning of time," he explained, "the entire universe existed as a single particle of energy and matter, of infinite power and infinite density. When that particle exploded, everything that issued forth from it, all of time, all of space, all of matter–all of it–the entire universe remained inextricably tied to that first particle. The theory goes that to control the Fuse is to control the universe."

He watched Daniel manipulating his shield until he suddenly let it blow itself out. "I'm controlling the universe?"

"In a limited sense. The universe is giving you control. It, however, is always in charge."

"But how can this Fuse be in my Aegis and every other Aegis all at the same time?"

"Well, I never promised that it wasn't complicated."

Now Daniel could see what he should have seen all along. "You're Keeper Torin, aren't you?"

The stranger's eyes sparkled. "Indeed I am," he said. "And I must say I haven't seen that particular Aegis in a very, very long time."

WAR OF WILLS

"His name was Indigo Cort," Tor Torin said. "He was a remarkable man; quite the rebel in many respects. He would never take no for an answer. Rather like yourself."

"How do you know this is his Aegis?" Daniel asked.

"Because it's chipped on one edge," he explained. "And I'm the one who did it when I wasn't much younger than you are now."

Daniel glanced down at the silver relic. Sure enough, there was a tiny, jagged chip on the rim that he'd never noticed before now. "What happened?"

Torin drifted toward the window and his memories from a lifetime ago. "A story for another time," he said.

Something wasn't quite adding up. "If this was his Aegis, how did he lose it? What happened to him?"

"He died trying to save a people who refused to be saved."

"I don't understand."

The Keeper considered his words carefully. "History," he said, "calls it the War of Wills, though in truth it was merely the first great relic war. It began over a hundred years ago, when a Sinja of unimaginable skill and learning, calling himself the Achorint, believed that he had finally decoded a deep-seated mystery left behind by a very ancient alien civilization that we have come to know as the Destronomers."

Daniel didn't recognize the name.

"At least, that's what we call them. Who they were and what they called themselves, we shall never know. What is certain is that they lived and died a billion years before humans were ever born. From what scholars have been able to piece together, the Destronomers were obsessed with trying to see into the future and change their own destiny if they didn't like what they found."

That seemed perfectly normal. "Wouldn't anyone want to do that?"

"Not like this," he said, finding Daniel's comment amusing. "They were consumed with changing not only their own fate, but the fate of everyone around them. Consider this," he said. "How would you react if you discovered that a mortal enemy were waiting to destroy you, yet neither of you had ever met–indeed this enemy hadn't even been born yet? What would you do with that knowledge? Do you try to understand them so that when they are born, you become friends instead of enemies? Or do you take the other route?"

It was a stunning idea. The perfect defense. "Destroy them before they are born," Daniel realized.

Torin took a moment to let the full importance of that sink in. "Yes," he said.

A horrifying thought suddenly reared up at Daniel. "The Sinja," he said. "If they gained control of this information . . ."

"They would become the most powerful force in the galaxy. Able to turn whole worlds against one another, purely on the off chance that what they pronounce might be the truth."

Torin stepped away, taking in the sight of his chambers as though it were to be the last time.

"The Destronomers realized their folly. That was why they dissembled their code and hid the parts throughout the galaxy. But millions of years passed, new civilizations emerged, the secret was learned, and every known intelligent race throughout the galaxy wiped themselves out of existence. Now here we are, and the Sinja want to repeat that conflict and bring about our own downfall . . . believing, as the Achorint did, that the Destronomers had discovered a fundamental truth, that everything that has happened, and everything that will happen, has been written into the very fabric of space itself. Like a blueprint. The

Sinja realized that if they could find all the missing pieces, they wouldn't just read that blueprint, they could physically rewrite it. Whole civilizations could simply cease to have been, on the whim of a Sinja. They could quite easily erase all of history as if it never happened. It has been my contention for some time that the Book of Planets is one such missing piece," Torin said. "We are the only ones with the power to stand in their way."

Daniel was still trying to wrap his mind around the whole idea. "How many other missing pieces are there?"

Torin threw up his arms. "Who knows?"

Torin drew closer. "A hundred years ago," he explained, "the Sinja thought they had found another piece of the Destronomers's legacy on a remote planet. The Achorint convinced the people of that world that the key to their power and prosperity lay right beneath their feet, hidden in the dirt. All they had to do was dig. And that's what they did, day after day, deeper and deeper, until slowly the entire planet was plundered. Even when the air was no longer breathable, and there wasn't enough vegetation to feed them, still they dug. We tried to warn them. We showed them the truth, that even if they did find what they had been promised, the Sinja were never going to let them keep it. They were being used. Exploited. But their minds were so willfully filled with mindless lies and endless propaganda that they didn't want to see the truth. They constructed enemies out of us, convincing themselves that we were the ones plotting their downfall by trying to stop them from unearthing their birthright."

Torin took a moment to steady his nerves, the raw emotion of his memory too much to bear.

"Indigo Cort," he said, "in a last-ditch effort to save them from themselves, took on a lone crusade, vowing to deny them access to whatever it was they thought they had found, hoping that would end it."

Daniel couldn't believe what he was hearing. "What happened?"

"They destroyed themselves anyway. One of the most verdant lands in all the galaxy, destroyed by greed and selfishness. All that's left now is a graveyard, a few rocks floating in space and five suns."

Five suns?

All this time Torin had been talking about the very planet Daniel had been imprisoned on in the relic mines. He glanced up at the Keeper. "The Sinja are still digging," he said. "And I was there . . . wasn't I?"

"The name of the planet was Musa Degh," Torin said, rubbing his furrowed brow in the seeming hope that he would ease his troubled mind.

Musa Degh? That couldn't be right. He'd seen the star charts, the trade routes. Hex told him that planet no longer existed. Everything indicated that there was just no way that the mines had been on that planet. Had the *WaKeenee*'s star charts been faked?

Ionica's wisdom rang in his ears: you can't find the truth by plugging your brain into a databank and being told what to think!

The sudden clatter of someone or something stumbling around outside the door to Torin's chambers drew their attention. Torin stepped immediately in front of Daniel as the door slid open.

But it was just Hex. The anatom hurried inside.

"Have you been out there this whole time?" said Daniel.

Hex made sure the door had closed behind him before clicking urgently.

"What do you mean? I don't know. I don't think so."

"Yes, yes," Torin interjected, a little irritated. "Would you mind translating? I'm afraid I don't speak creature."

"He wants to know if you brought the Book of Planets up here."

"Why would I do that, when there's a perfectly good . . ." Torin's voice trailed off as he grappled with the implication. "Wait. Why is he asking?"

"Because it's gone from its chamber," he said.

Daniel watched as the blood drained from Torin's face.

They raced back to the Vault, but there had been no misunderstanding. The podium upon which the Book of Planets usually sat was bare.

"This is all my fault," said Daniel.

"Unless there's something you're not telling me, never

blame yourself for the motives and actions of others."

"But what are we going to do?" Daniel implored.

"We will do nothing. You will return to your studies and mention this to no one," said Torin, his eyes darting from one corner of the Vault to the next, thinking, always thinking. "While I pursue the book's return, silence is our strongest ally now," he said, gently. "If the Guild of Truth cannot keep such a powerful artifact as the Book of Planets under lock and key, how can we protect whole worlds? The Sinja need chaos for their advantage. We will not give it to them."

But the secret was not theirs to keep, and the chaos was not theirs to control.

37

CRISIS OF TRUST

"All rise! All rise!"

With Truth Seekers and visitors crammed into every corner of the Forum, Daniel stood amid the crowd, blood draining from his face, his hands shaking, hoping that Ionica and Ben were too distracted with the proceedings to notice. In the weeks that had followed the theft, things had only gone from bad to worse. What started out as a murmur of frustration from Truth Seekers who had had their research with the Book of Planets interrupted grew into a cacophony of alarm as rumors began to surface on worlds many light-years away, rumors spread by the Sinja themselves, that it was they who now controlled that most powerful of relics.

Before long, swarms of delegates from a hundred

different worlds began arriving to press the Guild of Truth for answers. So many different types of humans, some with such bizarre shapes that they didn't look human at all. The Great Migration in all its glory, when humans had left a divided planet Earth and the planets that they chose to conquer followed those same loose alliances, based on language and culture. Add evolution to the mix and thousands of years, and here stood mankind, at the precipice of total divergence.

And the differences were only increasing.

Trust was a very fragile and precious thing in the galaxy, and with few assurances to give, eventually the only hope of maintaining it was to agree to a Truth Conference.

As the delegates made their way into the hall, the mood instantly began to change. Most Beacons had no idea why the delegates were coming here. They'd just started arriving, and they were angry. Tensions flared, and in no time at all the delegates began to argue with one another, with dignitaries from some worlds refusing to sit anywhere near the ambassadors of others.

Soon the atmosphere was so hostile that the Truth Watchmen began patrolling the aisles in order to keep the peace.

Ben looked like he couldn't believe what he was seeing. "Anyone want to tell me what the Fuse is going on?"

Guilt burned inside Daniel, but he kept quiet, relieved when Torin led a plethora of Guardians into the chamber to start the proceedings.

"This Forum is now in emergency session!" the Sergeant-at-Arms cried.

Two Truth Watchmen appeared at each doorway and barred the exits so that the business of the Forum could begin.

When everyone sat down, the murmur from the assembled delegates was in stark contrast to a normal Forum of Truth Seekers. These were politicians for the most part, people who were used to being loud.

Down on the podium, Torin appeared entirely unruffled. He looked over his notes in silence and coughed to himself, refusing to speak until the delegates were each paying their due attention.

When he was satisfied, he gazed out at the assembled delegates. "Who calls this emergency session?" he asked simply.

An older-looking man near the front, strongly built and wearing full-body armor, stood to face the bench. "I do," he declared loudly.

Torin nodded. "Let the record show General Tekez of the War Guild has called this emergency session."

The reaction this time was not limited to just the visiting delegates. The rumble of surprise swept through the ranks of Truth Seekers and Beacons alike.

"How much do you want to bet–"

"Ben Quick, we'll find out soon enough what this is all about. Now be quiet!" Astrid snapped.

A wave of disapproval swept down the rows of Beacons, but it wasn't aimed at Ben. It was aimed at Astrid instead.

Shhh!

Ben looked very proud of himself. "Yeah, shut up, Astrid," he said.

Astrid clenched her teeth shut before the overwhelming need to scream got the better of her.

Daniel had to fight not to laugh this time. Ionica just rolled her eyes.

When the small matter of procedure between a few delegates and the bench finally came to an end, General Tekez was asked to address the Forum directly.

The general's imposing voice carried a great weight. "Over the past few days," he announced, "the War Guild has been asked to supply troops to defend sixteen separate worlds. Planetary defenses have become compromised. Tactical information has leaked into the public domain. Rumors are rife–"

A Truth Seeker stepped forward at the back, raising his hand. "Point of Order, m'lords!"

"General Tekez," Torin asked. "Do you yield the floor?"

The general bowed his head. "I yield," he said.

The Truth Seeker, one Daniel didn't recognize, got quickly to the point. "Supply of troops is the War Guild's affair. There are strict protocols. Are we to believe that an emergency session was called on the basis of investigating a rumor?"

"It was not," General Tekez barked, quickly losing

patience. "I called this session on the basis of asking a question!"

Daniel knew what was coming. He felt sick. He glanced at his friends briefly. Their attention was entirely focused on the unfolding drama below and they were not prepared for what was about to come.

Torin looked over his documents, as though putting them in order, and drummed his fingers on the cold obsidian. He sighed.

Bracing himself, he said. "Ask your question, General."

Daniel could tell by the general's face that he'd rather not ask the question at all. But he was duty bound to do so.

However, just as he opened his mouth to speak, someone else jumped in and asked the question for him.

"Is it true," Ambassador Huku demanded from the floor, "that the Guild of Truth is no longer in possession of the Book of Planets?"

The wave of astonishment that such a question could even be asked swept through the ranks of the Truth Seekers with far more disbelief than it did through the delegates.

"They're crazy," said Ben.

"That could never happen," Ionica insisted. "It would spell chaos."

Daniel hung his head in shame. He couldn't watch.

When Daniel had faced the Book of Planets in the library, he had been intent on finding his friends in the Overseers' mines. But what he hadn't realized was that the device he was using was potentially devastating to the stability of the galaxy if it were to fall into the wrong hands. The Book of Planets could be used to give detailed insight into the weaknesses and strengths of every civilization.

The Guild of Truth had been a neutral keeper of the Book of Planets for generations, using it only for the love of knowledge and the disputes that knowledge could settle. But if the user had dark intentions, that same information gave the perfect blueprint from which to launch an invasion or sow lies and encourage conflict.

Whoever controlled the Book of Planets held sway over all worlds.

Without any warning, Ionica got to her feet. "Ambassador," she asked pointedly, "has something happened in the Bantu Worlds to make you believe that the circumstances of the Book have changed?"

Huku took offense. "Must I take questions–from a Beacon?"

"You must," Torin replied with conviction. "We are all Truth Seekers here."

"Very well. Many things have happened," Ambassador Huku exclaimed. "Where should I begin? With the Olmec forces building up on our Denebian border? Or the entire population that is missing on Skepsis?"

Another delegate shot up, pointing an accusing finger. "We are building up forces in that region, because you are building up forces!"

"That is a lie!"

A scuffle quickly broke out between the two delegations, stopping only when the closest Truth Watchmen jumped in to separate them.

"Delegates, please!" Juro the Doubting scolded from her seat at the bench. "Control yourselves! If you cannot conduct yourselves in a civil manner during these proceedings, we will have you removed from the chamber!"

It took a while longer for something resembling calm to return to the floor of the Forum, but when it did, Torin was keen to ask questions. Daniel could see that something about Ambassador Huku's remarks had caught his attention.

"Ambassador," Torin asked energetically, "did you say that everyone on Skepsis was missing?"

Ambassador Huku grew impatient. Drawing himself up to his full and considerable height, he said, "Thirty thousand minors completely vanished."

"What do they mine?"

"Not miners. Minors. Children."

Torin abruptly sat back in his chair, his face pale and haunted.

Ambassador Huku was surprised. "You've seen something like this before?"

"Yes, many years ago," the Truth Keeper admitted darkly. "On Musa Degh during the War of Wills."

The Forum quickly filled with the rumble of voices and

panic. Daniel watched as Torin met the gaze of everyone who had been at the secret meeting. Including him.

It didn't go unnoticed by Daniel's friends. Ben turned to him. "What's going on?" he asked.

Daniel wouldn't look him in the eye.

"With respect, Keeper Torin," General Tekez boomed over the din. "That is all well and good, but you have yet to answer our question. Is the Guild of Truth still keeper of the Book of Planets?"

"You must understand," said Torin, "I did what I thought was best, to prevent the very panic we see here today–"

Ambassador Huku thrust an accusing finger at all the Guardians. "Since when did guarding the truth mean hiding it? That book should have been destroyed long ago! It was a mistake to keep it!"

Up in the gallery, Ionica and Ben couldn't believe it. They turned on Daniel. "Did you know about this?"

"I wasn't allowed to tell anyone."

"For the last time, answer the question!" General Tekez roared. "Does the Fortress still hold the Book?"

A hush settled over the delegates and Truth Seekers alike as they waited for Torin's answer.

The Truth Keeper slowly surveyed the crowd. Daniel could see how conflicted he was, but just as General Tekez was duty bound to ask the question, so Torin was duty bound to answer it. He closed his eyes.

"It does not," he said.

The Forum exploded in a deafening uproar. Delegates jumped to their feet, shaking their fists. How could the Truth Guild have kept this a secret? They had betrayed their sacred oath! How could the Guild ever be trusted again?

The din of raised voices grew so loud, it was clear for all to see that the Truth Seekers had completely lost control of the Forum.

38
LEGACY OF THE DESTRONOMERS

That night, Tor Torin called a meeting in his chambers.

The room was filled with senior Truth Seekers, one or two of who Daniel even knew by name: severe faces, etched with worry. Ionica, who had asked to come if only to keep Daniel out of trouble, stood nervously by the window, her arms folded tightly across her chest.

Daniel didn't know what to make of it all.

"The Sinja," Torin commented, "lie as much to themselves as they do to others. Usually by now they're fighting among themselves for dominance."

"So what changed?" a fellow Truth Seeker demanded.

"Obviously they've found something," another one remarked; it was Raze Alioth, the tall, broad-shouldered Truth Guardian Daniel had seen arrest Darius Hun aboard the *WaKeenee.* "Mr. Coldstar, the mines that these–what did you call them, Overseers–had you working in? They had you searching for relics, correct?"

All eyes settled on Daniel.

"Yes, sir," he replied, unsettled by all the attention.

"Do you remember what they had you looking for?"

How could he forget? "Everything. Anything," Daniel explained. "There were a lot of diggers. A lot of relics."

"But nothing in particular? Thought Detonators have been turning up all over the place recently. Do they look familiar to you?"

Daniel shook his head. "Only the one Keeper Torin had . . ."

Torin rounded his desk, frantically trying to get Daniel not to say any more. Too late.

Daniel grimaced. "Sorry. You didn't tell me it was supposed to be a secret."

All eyes settled on Torin.

The Truth Keeper scratched his brow. Caught.

"Not a secret. I just didn't want anyone to know."

"Torin . . . ?" said Alioth.

"I'm the Truth Keeper," Torin replied, trying to brush it aside. "The Keeper of Relics."

"We agreed, no Thought Detonators–" Juro the Doubting cut in.

"How do you expect me to understand them, if I can't study them?"

"You can study them anywhere else in the galaxy, just not here!"

"Enough!"

Daniel recognized the strong, confident voice. He glanced around the room to find the Chief Verdicti from Toshka pushing her way to the front. She looked just like any other Truth Guardian now that her sleeks had changed back to their natural metallic gray color.

Torin hung his head. "Nice to see you, Morithia," he said. "Thank you for finding the time to attend at such short notice."

Daniel got the impression that he really wasn't saying thank you, and that she held an equally dim opinion of Keeper Torin.

"We're missing something," she mused. "The Sinja obviously sent this boy," she said, drawing everyone's attention back to Daniel, "as a diversion, to aid in their theft of the Book of Planets."

Daniel couldn't believe what he was hearing. "No one sent me! I escaped!"

"And I have no doubt that you believe that," she said, before addressing her peers. "But consider the trail of clues they have left behind, enough clues for us to follow a trail all the way back to them. Why? What have they found that they would be so confident we would be powerless against it?"

While the Truth Seekers bickered over the legends of

ancient artifacts scattered throughout the galaxy, Daniel sat down, his mind wandering back to that wretched place, back to that chamber filled with endless row upon row of . . .

"The armor," Daniel said quietly.

"What armor?" Ionica anxiously prodded, trying to keep her voice down too.

Daniel shrugged. "Enough to equip an entire army . . ."

It was only as he said it that Daniel realized the room had fallen silent.

"I know of no legend which talks of powers associated with ancient armor, alien or otherwise," Juro the Doubting remarked. "Do you, Torin?"

"Not armor, no," Torin replied, his mind obviously racing. Rummaging through his desk, he cleared a space and planted a document projector. Like petals on a flower, thousands of documents, suspended in the air, began unfolding all around him. Shuffling through them at a rapid pace, Keeper Torin quickly assembled his theory. "Here," he said, "the fall of the Arachnivores. The legends of the Esseed. The Mark. The Kittion. All speak of a remorseless force, an army of uncanny ability; the Esseed even believed that they were able to see the future, predicting the movements of their opponents before they had even thought of them themselves. Until one day they simply vanished."

"You're talking about the Lost Legion of the Mythrian Army," Alioth said.

Torin nodded. "What if it's not the soldiers themselves we should be worried about, but what they wore?"

Morithia refused to believe it. "The legends make it very clear that the Mythrians were a race with biological, alien abilities beyond our comprehension. Besides, no evidence has ever been found that they truly existed. No empire, no home world, no artifacts of any kind."

"And what if the legends are wrong? What if we know them under another name? What if these suits of armor that Daniel found are one more legacy of the destructive power of the Destronomers? Combine that strength with the Destronomer technology of the Book of Planets, and what do we have?"

"I don't believe it."

"It doesn't matter if you believe it. What matters is that the Sinja believe it."

"The Mythrian Army, unearthed on Musa Degh?"

"Why not?"

"Because if it's true," Morithia said, laying a gentle hand on Torin's arm, "an army that can see the future would be unstoppable."

FULL CIRCLE

The Equinox *and the* Azimuth *burst* out of Inspinity into orbit around Musa Degh.

"If the Sinja are on the surface, they're hiding their signals," Ben Quick said, checking the scopes for any signs of activity. "Scanning for ships."

Torin took his own look at the ship's instruments. He rubbed his chin thoughtfully. "Let's move in closer," he said. "But do it cautiously."

"If they can see the future," Daniel said, gazing out of the Sphere and watching the broken world of Musa Degh coming into view, "then they already know we're here and what we're about to do."

"And are you saying we should give up and go home?"

Daniel didn't know how to respond to that. Instead he

watched the world from which he had once escaped loom ever closer.

Bla-bleep. Bla-bleep.

Everyone around the Operations Bay glanced over at the REPIS scopes to see eight phantoms, jagged-edged Sinja starfighters, heading straight at them at blistering speed; hawks swooping in for the kill.

At least, they started out as eight. Within moments they multiplied like a disease, eight ships becoming sixteen, becoming thirty-two, becoming sixty-four.

The commlink crackled as the pilot of the *Azimuth* got in touch. "*Equinox*, are you seeing this?"

"Holocule decoys," Torin muttered.

"They're jamming our scopes," a Truth Seeker cried from the other side of the Sphere. "We can't tell decoys from real!"

A shadow crossed Torin's face. "Splinter the ship," he said.

The Truth Seekers jumped into action. Grabbing helmets from the racks, they tore out of the Sphere and hurtled down the long corridors.

Ben stopped only to say good-bye. "Good luck on the ground, Daniel."

Daniel appreciated it. "Good luck to you too."

Ben nodded, before racing off to his station.

Rrrrrmmmmm!

Heavy doors rumbled down behind them, cutting them off from the rest of the ship.

Ka-choom! Ka-choom!

The sound of locking clamps being released echoed around the cabin, followed by the whine of servo motors. The *Equinox* began to shudder while the cabin filled with a rumble so deafening that it seemed like the air itself had started to scream.

Shhhhwwweeeeiiiiii!

"Spitfires are powered up, engines are online," Ionica announced.

"Phantoms closing in!" Daniel said. "They're opening fire!"

Suddenly the Sphere lit up with rapid plasma blasts.

Tee-tee-tee-tee-tewwwwww!

The *Equinox*'s cannons whirred into action, ripping out a heavy retaliation.

Ch-tsooffff! Ch-tsooffff!

The *Equinox* shook so violently that Daniel was knocked off his feet. He glanced around to see every direction filling with the blinding fury of starfighter engines rocketing away.

SHWWWWWWWOOOOMMMM!

The deafening roar of the engines was so loud that Daniel could barely hear Ionica when she yelled: "Spitfires away!"

From out in space, four of the *Equinox*'s brightly colored long arms rocketed away from the main body of the ship, splitting in two as they went. For a brief moment it really did look like the *Equinox* had splintered into pieces.

But it was an illusion.

As the pieces separated, they quickly sprouted wings and armament pods.

These were *Equinox*'s Spitfires; eight Truth Seeker starfighters that she carried with her at all times. Their fuselages glinted in the bright light of Musa Degh's five suns. In a flash, they shot off in screaming pursuit of the Sinja attack ships, leaving the *Equinox* behind to provide covering fire.

Daniel ran to watch the battle unfold on the scopes. As the radio chatter grew louder and the pilots traded call signs and tactical moves, he followed their progress as projections of them whizzed around in front of him.

It was easy to see who was who and what was what; the REPIS computer labeled every craft, the words whizzed around with them, and the display was so accurate that the colors of the different ships could easily be seen.

Immediately Daniel spotted trouble. "Ben," he blurted, "behind you!"

There was a burst of interference and then Ben answered back, "I see him."

At the same time a Spitfire took evasive maneuvers across the REPIS, trying desperately to shake the Phantom from its tail. Arcing around, it sped toward the *Azimuth*, just as it too splintered.

A burst of light flared across space as all the *Azimuth*'s

own starfighters roared into battle and whipped around, locking on to the Phantom and charging straight at it, cannons blazing.

Ch-tsooffff! Ch-tsooffff!

The Sinja ship banked away but it didn't stand a chance. One good hit and . . . the starfighter evaporated. A holocule decoy drawing them away from the real attack.

Ben got straight on the commlink. "Thanks, *Yellow Tail.*"

"Spitfires, fall back!" another pilot ordered. "Don't get suckered."

The *Azimuth*'s starfighters, bulkier craft called Hurricanes, with greater firepower but not as fast as Spitfires, zipped toward the *Equinox* in pursuit of another target.

Daniel spun around to watch them through the window as they streaked past. His mouth hung open at the awesome sight of the eight Hurricanes speeding away, their yellow tail fins glinting from the glow of their engines.

Shhhhhwwoooommmmmm!

"Wow!" he cried.

"Well, well, well," said Torin as he analyzed the battle intensely. "Would you look at that?"

Daniel tuned back to the REPIS. "Look at what?" he asked.

"The Sinja can't stop lying, even in a fight," he said excitedly.

Daniel took a good look at the dogfight, but he couldn't see what Torin was talking about.

"There," Torin exclaimed, racing around to view the battle from another angle and excitedly pointing to an area on the edge of the map. "It's a diversion!"

Ionica's eyes lit up. "You're right," she said. "They're drawing us away from this area here."

"Then that's where we go," said Torin.

Orders started flying between the two splinter groups. The *Equinox* would head in. The *Azimuth* would cover them.

The Sinja realized that their plan had been foiled only when the Truth Seekers suddenly broke off their counterattack.

Coming around, the Phantoms regrouped into two deadlier formations, flying side by side, concentrating their firepower on one starfighter at a time, trying to pick off the slower ships first as they raced to catch up.

Tee-tee-tee-tee-tewwwwwww!

On the other side of the Sphere, Ionica had spotted a flow of incoming data that was too important to ignore. "We're picking up something under the surface," she announced.

"The mines," said Daniel confidently.

Was this it? Were his friends down there right now?

The commlink burst into life. "I'm hit!" the voice shrieked.

"*Azimuth* to *Yellow Tail Six*, we're on our way."

Daniel watched the situation unfold on the REPIS.

Hot plasma was leaking from the engine of *Yellow Tail Six* and the Hurricane had slowed to a limp.

The other Phantoms were closing in.

"We have to go back and help," said Daniel desperately.

"It'll be fine," Torin said calmly.

"But the *Azimuth*'s going the wrong way!"

"It will be fine, Daniel."

Just then the REPIS lit up as a bright explosion erupted from *Yellow Tail Six*. A tiny pinpoint of light blasted out from the starfighter at an angle.

Before Daniel even had a chance to figure out what it was, the Hurricane exploded in a shock wave, scattering the Phantoms into disarray.

Ionica sent a message through to the *Azimuth*, immediately asking for an update. It took a few moments for a reply to come back, but when it did the relief in the Truth Seeker's voice was obvious.

"We've got him, *Equinox*. Pilot retrieved."

Daniel couldn't believe it. "I don't understand," he said.

Torin thought it was obvious. "Ejector pod," he said. "It takes time and effort to train a Truth Seeker. What would be the point in letting one of us die?"

Daniel cocked his head. What was that noise?

Psssssshhhhhhhhhhh . . .

Ionica heard it too. "Everyone quiet!" she snapped.

Nobody argued. The sudden eerie silence in the Operations Bay unnerved Daniel more than the battle did.

Whatever the noise was, it was getting louder.

"Are we leaking atmosphere?" Daniel asked.

Sssssshhhhhhhhhhh . . .

Ionica checked the readings on her console. "No," she said. "Pressure's normal."

"Then what–"

KA-BLAM!

An explosion ripped through the *Equinox*'s hull. The screech of rending metal filled the cabin. Thick smoke poured into one of the corridors.

Truth Seekers across the sphere abandoned their stations in an instant, their Aegis shields springing up in a whirl.

Daniel's shield arm shook with fear. What was going on?

"We're being boarded!" Torin cried.

Dark figures jumped down through the ragged hull breech and advanced on the Truth Seekers. Electricity flared across the tips of their batons. Their rusted armor was wrapped in the stench of death and decay.

Overseers . . .

Ionica balled her fist and slammed an Aegis punch down the corridor at them to give the other Truth Seekers time to take up defensive positions.

The intruders staggered a little, but were not knocked off their feet as she had expected. Instead, they ran at the Truth Seekers without mercy.

Furious Truth Seekers unleashed on the Overseers, but still it did little to slow them down. Their armor was more effective against Truth Seeker attacks than even Torin had feared.

"I don't understand," said Daniel. "My attacks worked in the mines."

"Fall back!" Torin ordered. "Seal the Sphere!"

"No, we can do this!" Daniel insisted, running through the doorway at the Overseers, just as thick defensive doors thundered down behind him, sealing the Sphere off from the rest of the ship.

Ionica pounded on the door. "Are you crazy?!" she cried, but it was too late. She hammered on the controls, but they were shut off. She shot a look back at Keeper Torin. "Now what?"

Daniel stood alone against the Overseers, bracing himself for the inevitable attack, yet the Overseers refused to engage.

"Whatever your plan, it's not going to work," Daniel warned.

The Overseers did not respond. Instead, in perfect unison, they pulled back one by one to line the walls of the corridor, revealing a figure calmly watching from the other end of the corridor–a Sinja.

Daniel threw up his shield. "You won't win," he said defiantly.

"I already have, Dee," the Sinja replied, reaching up and removing his helmet.

Daniel couldn't believe his eyes. Shocked, he lowered his shield, unable to think clearly.

No one had called him that name in a long time.

This couldn't be real. It had to be a lie. It had to be. Yet the truth was staring him right in the face.

40

BACK FROM THE DEAD

The two friends stood at opposite ends of the *Equinox* corridor, facing off.

Blink Darkada . . . a Sinja? Impossible! Daniel pulled his hand back, readying his Aegis.

"You never came back for me, Dee," said Blink.

"What?" Daniel was caught completely off guard. "How can you say that?" he said. The last time he'd seen Blink Darkada, he was being snatched by a Nightwatcher. Nobody ever came back from that. "I thought you were dead."

"Do I look dead?" Blink asked.

"Well, I'm back now. And I'm here to rescue you–rescue all of us."

"Rescue me? Dee, I'm here to rescue you. Come with me."

Daniel's head started spinning.

Blink shook his head sadly. "What have they done to you?"

"Me? What about you?"

Blink didn't seem any different, though he must've been. Daniel knew Blink about as well as anyone could, or at least he thought he did. How had this happened?

The sound of heavy fighting from inside the Sphere grew louder.

Daniel glanced back to find Keeper Torin trying to get his attention, begging him to unlock the door.

Daniel eyed his old friend. Maybe there was a way to stop this. "Call off the Overseers and I'll come with you. It's that or we both die here and now."

Blink seemed agitated. He took a step forward. "You're making a mistake."

Daniel ignited his Aegis shield in a flash. "Prove me wrong," he said.

Blink clearly didn't like the idea, but he seemed to be thinking it over.

Trapped behind the shielded Sphere door, Torin thumbed the commlink. "Daniel!" he warned. "Don't trust him!"

"I have to do something," Daniel replied.

"Of course you do, just not this!"

Blink signaled the nearest Overseer. "Begin the retreat," he commanded. The Overseer nodded, signaling his troops to follow him out. Moments later, the sound of heavy fighting throughout the ship began to fade.

Alone with his old friend, Daniel said, "Thank you."

"Follow me," said Blink.

Daniel did as he was asked, leaving Torin's cries far behind him.

Blink's Phantom, docked where one of the *Equinox*'s starfighters used to be, had a sickly, musky smell to it. The dark cockpit, bathed in the red glow of its flight controls, had very little room beyond the pilot's seat.

Climbing down into it, Daniel remarked, "I don't think we're both going to fit."

"Both of us don't have to," Blink replied, disappearing in a cloud of holocule dust.

The cockpit sealed shut before Daniel could say anything, and the Phantom shot off into space.

Daniel slammed his head against the headrest. It was a holocule, not Blink! How many more times were the Sinja going to make him feel foolish?

Steering toward Musa Degh, the Phantom kept track of in-range targets with a series of crosshairs shooting around the cockpit window, calculating and recalculating its route down to the shattered world to avoid combat while the Truth Seekers and the Sinja continued to engage in their vicious battle.

"I'm sorry I couldn't be there to meet you in person. I'm glad you're okay," said Blink suddenly. "The Truth Seekers are bad people, Dee."

Daniel glanced around. The commlink on the flight controls had opened. "You don't know them the way I do," Daniel replied.

Blink scoffed. "Spoken like a true believer," he said. "Have you never wondered why they call themselves Truth Seekers?"

Daniel refused to answer.

"Because if they knew what the truth was, they wouldn't be looking for it. And if they don't know what the truth is, why would you trust anything they say?"

Daniel felt his skin crawl. He could taste bile rising from the pit of his stomach and burning his throat. There was logic to what Blink had said, and that was what frightened him the most.

No wonder Blink was blind to the truth. What other warped ideas had the Sinja filled his head with? Until Daniel knew more, convincing Blink of anything was going to be next to impossible, but he owed it to his friend to try.

"You're right about one thing," Daniel said. "I should have tried to save you. Maybe it's not too late."

Blink took a long while to reply. "It's never too late to do the right thing, Dee."

Blink clicked off without another word.

The Phantom shook violently as it swooped down into Musa Degh's hazy atmosphere. Daniel felt his ears pop as the pressure changed.

The planet seemed even more desolate than the last time

he was here. The craggy mountains were still dry and barren. A vast complex of rusting towers sat crowded on a plateau. Daniel could almost smell the oil and grease as they flew by.

Beyond the mining complex, the Phantom flew toward an enormous mine shaft that was perhaps more than a mile across. The rocky chasm plunged so deep into the ground that it didn't appear to have an end.

Shwooommm.

Without warning, the Phantom flipped down into the darkness.

"Ouch!"

It took Daniel a moment to realize that he hadn't been the one to say it. It came from behind. Someone else was inside the ship with him.

Cautiously, he peered over the back of the headrest.

"Ionica . . . ?"

41

WATCH YOUR TOESIES!

"How did you even get in here?" Daniel snapped.

Ionica grunted as she tried to wriggle out of the compartment she'd squeezed herself into. "You don't want to know," she said, struggling to free her leg.

Daniel checked the flight controls to make sure the Sinja weren't listening in on their conversation.

"What are you doing here?"

"Saving your butt. Again."

"They–my friend–or Sinja, whatever he is now–said they would call off the attack if I came alone."

"And you believed them?" Ionica replied, incredulous. "I'm glad I came." She glanced out the cockpit window at the delicate-looking gantries and muddy work platforms clinging precariously to the face of the mine shaft, spiraling down the inside for miles.

"Home sweet home," Daniel whispered, watching the shaft grow darker, the mining platforms lit up with clusters of work lights, exposing glittering honeycombed chambers—the mines he and Blink had spent much of their lives in.

How strange to be back.

"Looks like a welcoming committee," Ionica noted, indicating the reading on the Phantom's forward sensors. Thirty or so figures stood on a landing platform about two miles away. "You ready?"

"For what?"

"Watch your toesies!" she said.

Daniel glanced down at his feet, utterly confused. "What are you talking about?"

KA-BLAM! WHOOOSH!

The Phantom's cockpit glass blasted away from the ship, thanks in no small part to Ionica's deft touch with an Aegis.

"Take my hand," she said, and the two of them rocketed out into the frigid air of Musa Degh.

They landed amid the ruins on the planet's surface, running for cover before they were spotted by any passing Overseers.

"Now what's going to happen when that ship arrives and I'm not on it?" Daniel snapped.

"Who cares?"

"Who cares? That's your plan?"

Ionica made a run for it. "Come on, you want to save your friends or not?" she replied, weaving between columns and ducking into and out of small tunnel systems, Daniel closely following behind.

Dropping down to a lower expanse, they waited, listening for the telltale sounds of approaching company.

Daniel wrinkled his nose. "Overseer stink," he whispered.

Sprinting into the next corridor, Daniel didn't wait for Ionica to catch up; he ran at the squad of Overseers who were coming right at him, raised his arm, and–

Whompff!

Blasted them in every direction possible.

Ionica bounded over to get a close look at one of the bodies. "Weird," she said. "Do you have any idea where we're going?"

"This is your idea."

"But you used to live here."

"Right, and the first day you arrive as a prisoner, they hand you a map." Daniel took a deep breath, looking around for some kind of landmark he might recognize–nothing.

Ionica slid the palm of her hand through the air, bringing up a holographic display console. "Patching into the *Equinox*'s scopes," she said.

The familiar curved disk of the REPIS system in the Sphere projected out around Ionica. After a couple of rotations, a detailed map of the mines began to emerge.

Daniel homed in on the one thing that seemed all too familiar–a series of tall, thin structures in a cave that looked like a bed of crocked nails. "The Racks," he said. "That's where we used to sleep."

"That's quite the hike," Ionica pointed out. "It's a couple of miles away."

"Then we better get going."

Staying out of sight and avoiding patrols really slowed things down, but after a good hour or so they made it to a large hatch in the ground. This had to be where the Nightwatchers used to enter. Daniel heaved it open and peered over the edge.

There they were: the filthy beds that he and the grubs called home.

Without wasting any time, they dropped down into the Racks using a couple of quick bursts of energy to break the fall.

The familiar creak of the rusted bed frames echoed throughout the chamber. The Racks were empty, or at least, they seemed that way until–

A sneeze, brief and uncontrollably human.

"Bless you," Daniel whispered.

A voice, distant and confused, answered, "Daniel . . . ?"

Daniel peeked under the beds.

"Nails? Is that you?"

A couple of stacks away, a boy with fingernail hair lay trembling, facedown in the dirt. When he heard Daniel's familiar voice, he glanced up in awe.

"I don't believe it," Nails whispered.

They helped him up from his hideout.

"Did anyone else make it?" Daniel asked excitedly.

"A couple," Nails replied. "I think."

"What about Nova?"

Nails shook his head. "I haven't seen her."

"Where are the others you *do* know about?" Ionica insisted.

"I can take you to them."

"Let's go," she said, breaking into a run.

Nails ran after her, but Daniel did not follow. He'd spotted something that Ionica had missed, and not surprisingly, since it's not like she had ever been here before.

When they were far enough away, he activated his Aegis and brought an entire row of Racks crashing down, preventing them from doubling back.

Nails stopped dead in his tracks; glancing back, he spied the gleaming relic still affixed to Daniel's chest after all this time. "You've been practicing," he said.

"Go," Daniel urged.

Ionica was not happy. "Daniel, what are you doing?" she demanded.

"Get Nails out of here," he said. "Get everyone you can find out of here. I have to do this."

"Do what?"

"Rescue my friend."

And with that he stepped out into the open, and to where a squad of Overseers who had been hiding in the shadows emerged to escort him back to where Blink was waiting.

The Sinja were in control now.

42

HEART OF DARKNESS

They marched Daniel through the decrepit heart of Musa Degh; a cohort of towering Overseers surrounded him, and Blink was beside him every step of the way.

"Did anyone else survive the escape?" Daniel asked. "What about Fix?"

Blink seemed to hesitate before replying. "Some of them had destinies that were . . . unacceptable," he said.

What an odd thing to say. Now that really put a shiver down Daniel's spine. "What the heck is an unacceptable destiny?" he asked.

"You'll see," Blink replied coldly. "We're destined for great things, you and me, Dee," said Blink confidently. "I've seen it."

Daniel had never seen this part of the mines before. It

was filled with hissing pipes covered in frozen sheets of water vapor. Sizzling electricity arced from wall to wall above their heads. The air was cold and thin, but a musty smell reeked throughout the corridors.

When they reached a dead end, the floor shuddered gently before beginning its slow rise up to the next level.

When the platform came to a rest, Daniel found himself standing inside a very familiar cavern–the enormous armored dome he had encountered when he had first escaped the mines, with its multitude of holocules. Bolts of lightning arced across its surface, in step with the hissing pipes and the occasional breath of steam that made it seem as though it were alive–

What was that? A movement in the shadows . . .

All around the edge of the chamber, dark demonic figures stood watching him, their true faces hidden behind their masks–the Sinja were waiting.

"Well done, Acolyte," one of them whispered.

Blink stepped forward. "I told you he'd come," he said.

From the shadow of a parked Phantom starfighter, its cockpit glass long gone, a hatch in the fuselage creaked open, and a great lumbering hulk of an anatom came ambling out, its single misplaced horn all too familiar.

Hex A. Decimal made his way over to Blink and gently opened up his own chest cavity, revealing the Book of Planets that he had smuggled out of the Fortress of Truth.

"Hex . . . ?" Daniel whispered, unsure if what he was

witnessing was really happening.

With one oversize hand and a clumsy set of pincers, Hex lifted the weighty tome out of its hiding place and clutched it tightly. "I did warn you that going down to the Vault was a bad idea," the anatom said, refusing to look the boy in the eye.

The betrayal burned deep inside Daniel, creating a hole into which equal parts sorrow and anger had already begun to seep.

"You saved my life," said Daniel, confusion tearing at his voice.

"I saved my mission," the vexed anatom explained. He shuffled forward, but his legs seemed to move against his will. His hands trembled ever so slightly.

"I saved yours . . ." Daniel reminded him. "And for what? You were with them this whole time?"

Hex glanced up, his eyes glassy, the closest an anatom would ever come to weeping. "Without you as the perfect distraction, I would never have gained access to the Fortress of Truth," Hex explained. "I'm sorry."

"Bring the Book to me," one of the Sinja whispered.

Hex remained rooted to the spot, trying with all his might to refuse the command. His limbs stitched with the struggle.

"Hex," Daniel pleaded. "You have a choice."

But the anatom had already lost his battle. "No, I don't," Hex replied, lurching forward, doing what he had been programmed to do: delivering the prize to his master.

The Sinja held the hefty tome reverently. "Vega Seftis will be pleased that the next phase of his plan can commence," he said.

"I'm so glad," Daniel said. "I was beginning to worry you'd all let him down."

The Sinja handed the Book back to Hex. "Place it into the chronoscope."

The anatom did as he was commanded.

"Do you know who I am, boy?" the Sinja asked, stepping into the light.

Yes, he knew him, the dark Sinja he had battled in holocule form. But Daniel wasn't about to give him the satisfaction. "Not a clue," he said.

"I am Vega Virrus," he whispered darkly. "And I have brought you home. And to make you comfortable, I have brought the two things here that you cherish the most."

He meant Blink and Hex. But home? This place was many things, but it was not home.

More crackling electricity sparked across the chamber, causing the frozen pipes to hiss, vaporizing patches of ice into instant steam.

"Come," the Sinja commanded.

"Get lost," Daniel replied.

An Overseer shoved him roughly from behind. Daniel fell forward but stayed on his feet. He glanced over his shoulder. "Yeah, I missed you too," he said.

The Overseer went to jab him again, but Blink blocked his way. "No, wait!" he barked.

There was the Blink Darkada that Daniel knew. He smiled to himself, but the glimmer of hope was short-lived.

"I've seen my future, Dee," Blink explained. "I've seen yours too. They have it all mapped out. It's glorious! All you have to do is look." He gestured to the gigantic metal dome, where Hex was loading the Book of Planets into its central core.

Daniel watched, stunned, as the Book floated in a column of light, spinning on its axis, surrendering every star and planet in its knowledge bank.

"What did you see when you saw your future?" Daniel asked, not sure that he really wanted to know the answer.

Blink rolled his shoulders back proudly. "They showed me who I was born to be, Dee. One of the most powerful Sinja who ever lived!"

Daniel couldn't hide his disgust. "What are you saying? We were their prisoners, don't you remember the mines?"

"They were testing us. Don't you see? They were making us stronger."

Daniel felt the impulse to run deep in his gut. "No," he said, edging back.

Vega Virrus had waited long enough. Impatiently, he strode toward the machine, signaling the Overseers. "Since you will not go willingly," he said, "we will persuade you. Bring him!"

The Overseers lurched forward to do his bidding, grabbing Daniel roughly by the arms and dragging him across the chamber. Daniel jammed his heels down, but it was no use. They were too strong.

When the Overseers eventually released Daniel, despite being outnumbered he wasted no time in pulling his hand back to ready his Aegis.

The Sinja made no move toward his own weapon. "Unwise," he said. "Thought Detonators are everywhere. . . ."

Daniel's hand trembled. Was the Sinja lying or telling the truth? Only one way to find out: call his bluff–

His Aegis refused to function.

Daniel panicked. He glanced down; did he still even have it? Yes, there it was, sitting where it had always been, gleaming over his heart. Why didn't it work?

"It seems your heart and head do not agree," Vega Virrus hissed.

Daniel looked away. With Blink in the room, if he attacked now he'd have to face his friend in battle, and Daniel knew he wasn't ready to do that.

Regardless, Daniel tried again. Without success.

Vega Virrus turned his back on Daniel, as if to show that the boy was no threat, and moved toward the controls of the machine; what did he call it–the chronoscope?

"The Aegis, much like the Truth Seekers, is a limited weapon. It requires total obedience. My weapon is superior.

It has no such limitations." Virrus turned on Daniel. "You should not be a slave to your limits either. You have a great destiny, Daniel Coldstar, if you will only accept it."

Daniel felt it in his chest first, the nervous energy that told him that his uncertainty was only growing.

"Just look, Daniel," Blink urged from the shadows.

Daniel swallowed hard. This was a bad idea, but what other choice did he have? Besides, this way he'd at least have some understanding of what they had done to Blink. Assuming he made it out of this with his mind intact.

"Show me," he said quietly.

Daniel took a deep breath, expecting some kind of mind-altering delusion to suddenly fill his senses, or find his soul being sucked from his body, but he experienced none of that. Instead, he heard a voice approaching from around the other side of the chronoscope.

"Daniel?" it said.

It took a moment to process, but Daniel realized he was listening to his own voice.

He watched as a ghostly holocule version of himself came circling toward him, bearing a twisted Askarai on his chest, and wearing the armor of an Overseer.

BENEATH THE MASK

"Who are you?" asked Daniel nervously.

"Who do you think I am?" Sinja-Daniel replied. "I'm you. I'm your future."

"I don't believe you."

"Belief doesn't matter."

"I destroyed you."

"You can't destroy your future, only variations of it."

Sinja-Daniel tapped the power of his Askarai, sprouting huge bat-like wings, propelling himself up into the air.

"You're the greatest Sinja who ever lived!" Sinja-Daniel exclaimed. "Never to be a slave, never to be bullied. You will never be weak. Worlds will bow at your feet, for you are destined to be respected and feared!"

In his gut Daniel knew this was wrong. But seeing

himself as a Sinja, as he would become–it seemed so real. So final.

Was this really who he was meant to be?

Think, Daniel. Think. Go back to the basic lessons.

"Why would I want to be feared?" Daniel asked.

Unable to answer, Sinja-Daniel disappeared in a puff of holocule dust, to be replaced by a kinder, gentler Sinja-Daniel walking toward him. "This power is yours, Daniel. All you have to do is claim it like your friends have claimed it."

"One friend," Daniel pointed out calmly.

Sinja-Daniel shook his head. He glanced over at the nearest Overseer. "Show him."

With electrical discharges rippling across the outer surface of the giant machine, a clanking Mythrian soldier did as it was instructed, came to stand in front of Daniel, and with little fanfare, lifted its face mask.

Actual flesh and blood, and not some holocule, looked back at him. The face of Nova, the girl who had been so kind to him when he'd been thrown in the pit. The girl who had been so upset that he couldn't remember who she was.

Somewhere deep down, Daniel had hoped that she had managed to escape just as he had, and was off somewhere having her own adventures.

The terrible truth crushed his soul instead.

"Hello, Daniel," she said.

Daniel swayed, his legs weaker than they had been a moment ago. "This is a trick."

Blink Darkada stepped out of the shadows to join him. "No trick. This is what we were bred for. This is why we exist, Dee."

"No."

"You can't just close your eyes and pretend this isn't happening–"

"No! No! No!" Daniel covered his ears, trying to escape their words.

Whompff!

A powerful shock wave blasted through the chamber, sending the Book of Planets clattering to the ground. Another Truth Seeker–

"Show me my future, Virrus!" a distant voice cried.

Everyone looked up to see Torin standing atop the machine, glaring down at them.

With the element of surprise still with him, he dropped down to the floor, his own Aegis shield a glowing disk of fire.

"Occator Torin," Vega Virrus whispered with excitement. "It's been too long."

"Only my mother calls me Occator," Torin snapped. "And she isn't here." He glanced briefly toward Daniel. "At least, I hope she isn't here," he said quietly.

Torin let his shield of fire die. He pulled a small device from his utility belt and held it up for them all to see.

Daniel recognized it immediately. It was the same Thought Detonator that Torin had been studying when they first met.

With one firm click, he armed it.

"Force me to defend myself, Virrus," said Torin, his eyes settling on the gigantic machine, "and you will regret it." He gave Daniel the briefest of sideways glances. "Get out of here, Daniel," he commanded. "They're not going to do anything. They wouldn't dare."

"You can't," Daniel warned.

"Just go. I have this–"

"You can't!" Daniel cried. "These are my friends."

"What are you talking about?"

Vega Virrus began to laugh.

"The Mythrian Army. Look at them!" Daniel pleaded.

The chamber filled with the sound of marching boots. Rank and file, rank and file, foot soldiers of the Mythrian Army on parade, the faceplates on their helmets lifted to expose the faces of one after another.

Dathan Tantus.

Kree Kalamath.

Ogle Kog.

Gungy Wamp.

Mymon Ray.

Dakan Liss.

One by one.

On and on.

Their faces drained of all humanity; the Sinja's children of war.

Coming to an abrupt halt, the Mythrian Army turned

on its heels to face the Truth Seekers.

"My God . . ." Torin gasped. He opened his commlink, quietly broadcasting to every Truth Seeker within range, "Do not engage."

"Is that fear I smell, Torin?" Virrus whispered, gathering his child army around him like a shield.

"I will not be party to the murder of children," Torin said, backing away.

"Yet you bring your own young ones into battle," Vega Virrus whispered.

Torin began to anger. "They are not soldiers," he said. "And they never will be." He added into his commlink, "Retreat. Now."

"We can't leave them!" Daniel protested. "We were supposed to free them!"

"We have no choice."

Vega Virrus's amused voice slithered around Daniel's scalp from one ear to the other. "Now do you see who they really are, Daniel? Powerless. Hypocrites. I stand within striking distance and they do nothing–"

Angrily, Daniel pulled his arm back to launch his Aegis, but Torin was faster. Gripping him by the wrist, he said gently but firmly, "No, Daniel."

Daniel struggled to snatch his arm away.

"I promise you, there will be another way," Torin implored.

But Daniel refused to give in. He turned back to Nova.

"Come with us," he begged. "You can be free!"

Nova simply gazed at him as though he were speaking an unknown language.

He turned to Gungy Wamp, to Dakan Liss, to any number of grubs. "Come with us!" he cried, over and over, until the tears stained his cheeks and his voice grew hoarse. "Come with us!"

"If you insist," Vega Virrus whispered. "Troops–attack."

And with that the dark Sinja unleashed the chaos that he so craved.

Daniel braced himself for the assault, but it never came.

The deafening sound of weapons fire filled the chamber as the Mythrian Army rushed at him, but Torin was having none of it.

Grabbing Daniel by the sleeks, Torin ignited his Aegis, focusing an almighty blast at the ground beneath their feet.

Whompff!

The two Truth Seekers shot up into the air so blisteringly fast that they looked for all the world like a bolt of lightning.

"The Thought Detonator!" Daniel cried in a panic, expecting a blast to erupt at any moment.

"Never worked," Torin replied. "You of all people should have remembered that!"

Careening through the same opening that Torin had used to make his entrance, the two tumbled into a smaller chamber, a passageway of sorts. Together, they landed at a run.

"You lied?" Daniel said, shocked.

"I did no such thing," Torin objected. "I invited them to infer. Never once did I state that the thing in my hand was any kind of threat."

PewPewPewPew!

The weapons fire coming from far below them zipped up through the opening near their feet, blasting everything to smithereens.

"I'm not sure this is the safest place to continue this conversation," Torin mused.

"Over here!" a familiar voice beckoned.

They spun around. At the very end of the passageway, where it began sloping up to the surface, stood Ionica. Behind her, three grubs wearing ordinary dugs: Nails, Henegan Rann, and Fix Suncharge. Behind them–Alice!

Daniel's heart thumped proudly. All had not been lost.

Before long they had caught up with the rest of the Truth Seekers, and were back aboard the *Equinox.*

From the Sphere, they watched the scene unfolding down on the surface of Musa Degh, legions of Mythrian troops lining up to board a fleet of gigantic ships the likes of which they had never seen, shaking off the dirt and rising up out of the graves they had lain in for a million years.

And there was absolutely nothing the Truth Seekers could do. At least not today.

"They were testing us," Torin said. "That's why they led us here. They wanted to know what we would do when faced with such an enemy. And now that they know, they will make a next move."

"Those ships, sir. They're scrambling our ability to track them," one of the Truth Seekers announced from her post.

Not to worry.

Daniel's heart, hidden under that nicked piece of ancient metal, was speaking to him in ways that the Truth Seeker training had taught him to recognize.

This was not the end. When the next move came–they would know.

44

THE SEVENTH SUMMIT

Daniel set out across the grasslands one afternoon, heading for a loosely wooded area hugging the ridge of the hills. The leaves had all started turning a brilliant shade of orange, and began falling in sheets like rain every time the wind blew.

"They're called seasons," Daniel explained, tugging on Alice's leash, guiding him around a steep curve. "This one is the fall. I read about it."

Alice bent his head down and nuzzled Daniel's ear, making him chuckle. "Cut it out."

As they made their way up to the crest of the hill, Daniel filled his lungs with the fresh scent of oozing sap and fallen leaves. When they emerged on the other side of the woods, he saw the charred ruins of what remained of the Seventh Summit.

At the river's edge they crossed an old narrow bridge over

to the far side, watching the brightly colored fish jumping in and out of the surging water. It was starting to get dark.

When they made it to the top, a small light could be seen glowing through the window of one of the intact upper floors.

Daniel hitched Alice to a post and began unloading the supplies: food, bedding, water. It would do for now.

A small glass card fell out of the bundle, skittering across the soil.

Daniel scooped it up, and as he did so, a message scrolled across its surface.

Daniel,

Welcome home. Remember, we are family now. Us Truth Seekers must stick together! And to that end, let me give you a little piece of advice that has always served me well: Always seek the truth. Guard it when you find it. Give it when it is most needed.

We will free them in the end, you know. And it will be glorious!

Until then, to the adventure, Daniel. To the adventure!

Your friend,

Torin

"Mind if we join you?"

Startled, Daniel glanced up to find Ionica and Ben standing across from him, heavy packs fastened to their backs.

"What are you doing here?" he asked.

"Moving in," Ionica said, looking for a decent entrance. "What about you?"

Ben shrugged. "Are you going to argue with her?"

Daniel shook his head. What was the point? "You're going the wrong way," he said.

With the bundle of supplies slung over his shoulder, Daniel led the way up the ragged stairs. The ruins had such an eerie feeling about them. As though the spirits of the dead were watching, reminding them all of the sorrow that had been wrought here.

"We don't have to live here, you know. We do have space back at the other summits," Ionica said.

"I know," Daniel replied simply.

When they reached the top, Daniel nodded to the others huddled around an open fire: Nails, Henegan, and Fix, all free thanks mostly to Ionica. Unlike their other friends still trapped in a web of lies a trillion miles away.

The three boys nodded in return when they saw him, enjoying their first night of freedom. Ionica nudged one of them to make room for her around the fire. Ben passed out the supplies.

And Daniel? He saw the sign the boys had painted on the wall. And he smiled.

Who disturbs?

We do.

Outside, in the valleys of Orpheus Core, a lone Hammertail roared.

GLOSSARY

The following entries have been retrieved from the *Encyclopedia Exodussica, 10th Edition.*

AEGIS: An Aegis (plural: Aegi) is an ancient weapon of unknown alien design. Each Aegis is unique, created from starflakes, crystals thrown from the solid cores of exploding stars. The theoretical principle behind the Aegis is that every particle in the known universe is still fundamentally attached to the original single particle from which the universe was created, known as the Fusion Point, or Fuse. Theoretically, no corner of the universe is immune to the effects of an Aegis, although in practice there do appear to be limitations. The discovery of the first Aegis in 8470 EE, and the resulting hunt for similar relics, led directly to one of the bloodiest relic wars in human history, the Edge Wars. VOL. 258.042

ANATOM: An anatom is an artificial life-form comprised of two parts: the corposum, or biological element, which is created from artificial DNA and which serves as the basis for its brain; and a mechanical outer shell, usually taking the form of an animal or animal-mechanical hybrid, though exceptions do exist. The enduring popularity of old-fashioned robots has seen anatoms, first created in 7133 EE as a replacement for robotic servants, often working alongside and complementing their counterparts, rather than replacing them.
VOL. 671.099

BLAST-PIKE: Blast-pikes are long, spear-like martial weapons designed for close hand-to-hand combat. Blast-pikes use S31 quadrocells as a power source and emit high-powered electrical discharges to both stun an opponent and physically remove or "blast" them away from the immediate vicinity.
VOL. 991.433

BURN WORLDS: Burn Worlds are any number of inhabited planets scattered throughout the galaxy with extreme, usually hot, environments. Most Burn Worlds orbit close to their parent star or stars, though some possess overheated, smog-like atmospheres filled with toxins due to human industrial activity. The Burn Worlds are not a single star nation, as is often assumed. Individual Burn Worlds exist in almost every alliance throughout the galaxy.
VOL. 992.643

CHAFF: Chaff is the language of Juke roamers.
VOL. 598.603

DROTE: Drotes are medium-sized, long-tailed rodents of the superfamily Randominus, within the order Rodentia. Varieties of drote include the common hairless drote (*Calvus drottus*) and spitting drote (*Sputo drottus*). Debate still rages among scientists on the origin of drotes. They were first recorded in 2127 EE when they ransacked the food storage units of the Alnair colonies, leading to the Alnair famine of the same year, in which 53,781 colonists are known to have perished. Drotes evolve rapidly and can adapt to wildly different environments in a single generation. Though genetically related to rats, beavers, and other rodents, modern drotes bear limited resemblance to their ancestors and are known for their aggressive temperament.
VOL. 781.001

EMBERS: The Embers are a series of planets that fell under Sinja control toward the end of the War of Wills. By appealing to fear and greed in the people, the Sinja convinced each population to relentlessly hunt for more relics within their territories, resulting in the destruction of their respective worlds. For decades after, the burning remnants of these planets in the night sky, which resembled the scattered remains of a dying fire, came to be known as the Embers.
VOL. 1012.027

ENGINOID: Enginoids, also known as Combines, are a class of robot whereby clusters of individual units work together as a single unit to accomplish tasks. The number of units in an enginoid cluster is determined by the assigned task. Enginoid clusters are highly configurable and self-sufficient.
VOL. 998.802

F-LIGHT: F-lights, or Floating Lights, are small, flying flashlights designed to allow a user to use both hands while performing a task. Voice commands may also direct an F-light to illuminate an area that would normally be out of reach.
VOL. 1265.055

GOLOADER: GoLoaders are a form of hover transport consisting of self-organizing, individually powered cargo containers that use antigravity repulsor units as their method of flight. Older models such as the TRS-80, manufactured by the now-defunct Fortran Corporation, employ booster cars or assist units in the front and back positions as added power when the containers travel in trains. Newer models such as Spectrum's ZX81 and Commodore's VIC 20 make use of Amiga technology and require no assist units.
VOL. 1773.817

HAMMERTAIL: Hammertails are a large quadruped form of trabasaur, noted for their armored skin and massive tail club. Hammertails were designed to resemble

ankylosaurid-type dinosaurs that roamed ancient Earth during the Cretaceous Period, which began and ended 145–66 million years ago.
VOL. 2850.013

JARABIC: Jarabic is a fusion language of the fourth millennium EE and is spoken by 1.3 billion people over a wide swath of the galaxy, primarily on the worlds of the Jeddaration, but also on some Bantu Worlds, the Sovo Compliance, the Raider territories, and several independent systems. Jarabic has its roots in both the Japonic and Semitic language families.
VOL. 4187.663

KOIN: Koin is the language of trade and is the most commonly used language in the galaxy. The majority of societies that use a different primary language still speak, or at least understand, Koin.
VOL. 9981.701

MENDESE: Mendese is an artificial Click language created to allow anatoms, enginoids, and other service automatons to communicate with one another without compromising the security of their internal systems. Mendese consists of a series of clicks and pops usually made with the tongue, and therefore does not have an alphabet. Mendese was inspired by the Click languages of ancient Earth, including the San People of the Kalahari Desert. Local Click

language dialects are still used on some remote worlds.
VOL. 22380.672

MUSA DEGH: Musa Degh was a minor planet that fell under Sinja control during the War of Wills, and subsequently destroyed by its own people due to blind greed. The fiery remains of Musa Degh were visible as part of the Embers for some twenty years after its demise. Nothing more remains of the planet today.
VOL. 38604.005

ORPHEUS CORE: RESTRICTED: YOU DO NOT HAVE SUFFICIENT SECURITY PRIVILEGES.
VOL. 41776.91

SPLINTERSHIP: Splinterships are interstellar spacecraft that carry a complement of smaller craft with them, integrated into the main fuselage until it is time to launch them. From a distance, the ship appears to "splinter" or break apart. Splinterships have many advantages over regular interstellar craft, the most notable being that the act of splintering confuses enemy targeting systems, giving the smaller craft, such as starfighters, the edge in leading a counterattack. Splintership designs are many and varied.
VOL. 59861.239

TRABASAUR: Any one of a number of species of work animal designed, genetically engineered, and bred for use in heavy labor. Trabasaurs distinguish themselves from other animals in that they can operate in diverse harsh environments without modification, and survive on minimal food and water. Superficially, trabasaurs often resemble dinosaurs, although this is purely cosmetic; trabasaurs are not genetically related to them.

VOL. 78772.348

TRUTH SEEKERS: RESTRICTED:
YOU DO NOT HAVE SUFFICIENT
SECURITY PRIVILEGES.

VOL. 79665.003

ACKNOWLEDGMENTS

THANKS

Lori, Dean, Shannon, Doug, Tweeze, Jenny, Marty,

Christina, Ed,

Debbie, Dan, Steven, Row, & Mum.

SPECIAL THANKS TO MY
TRUTH SEEKERS

Lorelai, Miss Jill, Miss Diana, Kate, & Nate.

READ ON FOR A
SNEAK PEEK AT THE NEXT
DANIEL COLDSTAR
ADVENTURE

1

A MAP OF HOPE

Nobody came here by choice. Now Daniel Coldstar knew why.

In the steamy Death Jungles of Oota Mheen, fifteen species of plant were poisonous to the touch. Thirty-seven types of bug could either sting, bite, or burrow their way into his brain. In every direction, massive tree trunks stood twisted together, while creeping vines strangled them, reaching all the way up to the branches overhead and forming impenetrable walls of black vegetation. Vicious eyes bored into him from creatures who sat crouched hidden in the dense foliage, waiting to pounce.

Everything was out to get him.

Daniel waded ankle-deep through lead-colored water, struggling to pull his feet from the sucking mud, when he heard a heavy *splash!*

Out of the corner of his eye he saw something slug-colored slither out of a nightmare and into the swamp.

What was that?

Waves rippled out toward Daniel. Poisonous algae swirled around his legs: akahana, toxic to humans and the best way to get blood to squirt from your eyeballs if swallowed. A minor inconvenience compared to fighting off an attack, but if that thing pulled him down into the water?

Maybe better to avoid a fight altogether.

Daniel held his breath. He stood perfectly still and waited for the creature to pass, sweat trickling down the back of his neck. The thick, heavy air burned in his throat–

Roaaar-kha-kha . . . ! Roaaar-kha-kha . . . !

The howl of a Jaranjar, what the locals called tiger-apes, echoed through distant treetops. Daniel sure hoped it wasn't coming this way, because that was all he needed right now.

Where did that thing in the water go?

There, its back arching as it surfaced. It headed in the other direction.

Daniel let himself take a breath.

"Maybe Nails was right," he said to himself. "Maybe this *is* a trap." He glanced around, wondering what options he had left. If he went back now, Ben and Ionica and all the other Truth Seekers would never know he'd been gone, but he'd never get his answer.

Waving his hand in an arc in front of his body, Daniel called up his holographic display. A map quickly projected out in the air around him. Ahead and behind, a series of glowing orbs snaked their way through the undergrowth. Red, showing where he had been; blue showing where he needed to go.

He trudged on, making his way up onto drier land where brittle twigs snapped underfoot; oblivious to a small metal flipper silently reaching out from the bushes.

It tapped him on the leg.

Daniel instinctively pulled his hand up, readying his Aegis. It was the weapon of a Truth Seeker. Ancient and powerful, a relic crafted by an unknown alien intelligence and forged from a single starflake, a crystal formed at the heart of a sun. The weapon vibrated faintly on his chest, listening to Daniel's thoughts, eager to bend all matter and energy into a powerful shield around its master.

But it was a false alarm.

"Will you stop doing that?" Daniel snapped. "I could have blasted you to pieces."

A few feet away, a nervous mechanical penguin bobbed from one webbed foot to the other. Its tritanium beak snapped shut like a steel trap while its crest of yellow light-wire feathers twitched disapprovingly over each eye.

"Don't give me that look," said Daniel. "It's not my fault Astrid didn't program you for speech."

The anatom, a cyborg fusion of machine and artificial life, puffed out his chest and extended his neck.

"Jasper . . . ," Daniel said, "I'm warning you–"

Jasper tilted his head, then gagged.

"Ugh, that's revolting!" Daniel agreed, cupping a hand

over his nose. "I think something died."

Jasper waddled off in search of the source. Humming.

Great anatom design, Astrid, Daniel thought. *Can't speak Mendes, but can hold a tune.*

Astrid Always. Always Astrid, always right. That was how she described herself. Constantly. She had a truly brilliant mind wrapped in an irritating personality. No doubt she had good reason for how she had programmed Jasper. She had just neglected to tell anyone, including Daniel, what that reason was.

Daniel hadn't known it at the time, but the first moment he met Astrid, she was already hard at work building Jasper aboard the *Equinox.* Of course, Daniel had had other concerns back then. Like his damaged traveling companion, an anatom named Hex. The rat had needed an entirely new exosuit and wound up wearing a mishmash of spare parts.

In retrospect, Daniel wished Hex had remained a rat. Maybe it would have made it easier to identify him as the betrayer he had turned out to be. Daniel hadn't quite trusted anatoms since then. Not even Jasper.

"I'm not sure this is a good idea," Daniel warned, reluctantly tagging along behind the penguin until their way was blocked by a dense mesh of leaves and vines that seemed to come in at least three different shades of black.

Daniel had never stepped foot on a planet that orbited a red dwarf before now. Here on Oota Mheen, the vegetation had evolved to absorb every ray of the star's weak sunlight by turning black instead of green. It looked as though shadows had become living things. It took some getting used to, not only because it looked so strange, but because–

The leaves rustled. Something was coming toward them. Something big, something so huge that it didn't care one bit about the supposedly impenetrable barrier of dense foliage.

Please don't be a Jaranjar. Please . . .

Its muzzle emerged first, a gigantic mouth set wide beneath wet, twitching nostrils. Forcing its way through, the rest of its gigantic head soon followed. Its face contorted as though it was uncomfortable. Then it farted.

"Eww, *really*?" Daniel now had *both* hands cupped over his nose. "This is where you went? What did I teach you about going downwind? No wonder that thing back there decided to go for a swim. Thanks a lot!"

For his part, Alice the Hammertail looked very pleased with himself.

Daniel tugged on Alice's reins, coaxing the massive trabasaur out into the open. Trabasaurs came in all sorts of shapes and sizes. In class, Daniel had learned that these work beasts were originally genetically engineered to resemble the dinosaurs of olden times. Alice had a gigantic spiked hammer on the end of his tail, perfect for smashing things.

Alice liked to smash things.

"You couldn't go a little farther away? I told you to drink more water, but no, you had to get backed up for three days."

Jasper angrily raised a flipper, eager to chop Alice in the knee. Alice raised an irritated foot, ready to crush the annoying little robot.

"Cut it out, the pair of you!" Daniel scolded. "We're not done here yet. Come on!"

They trekked on for another hour, listening to the buzz of insects and the chirp of things that kind of looked like birds. They had wings but they didn't have feathers. They had what looked like beaks, except they weren't, they were teeth all nested together, and Daniel only found this out when one of them dived at him and snapped at his face.

Though Daniel would never admit to it, having Alice here was a comfort. Not even a fresh mind wipe had managed to break the bond the two of them had formed back in the Sinja's relic mines.

The relic mines. Where he'd discovered his Aegis, the relic now attached to his chest, and won his freedom. That was over a year ago–had it really been so long? So much had happened since then.

Daniel took what he thought was going to be another careful step, but Alice gently nudged him out of the way.

The unfurled drab green petals of a trap-bloom lay stretched out on the forest floor. These plants were carnivorous, sitting open-mouthed on the ground for as long as it took for something tasty to wander through and then–*snap!* Lunchtime.

Daniel gave the Hammertail a thankful pat on the shoulder before checking the map one last time. "This is it," he said, "right over there."

He took a deep breath and hesitated.

Either he was about to uncover the first major clue in figuring out who he was and where he came from. Or he had been lied to. Again.

The trees parted like curtains as Alice forced his way through. Cautiously, Daniel kept one step behind him, and Jasper behind him, picking their way over the warped stumps until the three of them emerged together into a clearing bowled at the foot of a steep hill.

It took a moment for Daniel to truly grasp the enormity of what he was seeing. At first it looked like a natural formation, a rocky outcropping covered in growth. But look closer, and there were gaping black holes that used to be windows. Trees grew between exposed metal ribs, tall enough to hide much of the hull. Moss cascaded down the letters emblazoned across its bow.

This was a starship, lying on its broken back, engines in the air.

This is it! This is really it!

Whoever had sent him the map had been telling the truth.

There *was* a crashed ship on Oota Mheen, and its name was *Coldstar.*

THE MYSTERIOUS SHIP

Muscles rippled along Alice's back as he heaved at the vines Daniel had tied to the trabasaur's saddle. Thick festoons of vegetation slowly peeled away from the ship to expose its rotting hull.

The starliner moaned miserably from deep within as though the creepers had been the only thing holding it together. Daniel was going to find a way inside this ship even if he had to tear a hole–

Alice lurched forward and the aging metal screamed.

The great tangle of vines snapped taut. Then a large strip of twisted hull metal tore away from the wreckage and tumbled to the ground, leaving behind a gaping hole big enough for Daniel to climb through–if he could get up there.

"That works," Daniel remarked, chopping the vines from where he'd tied them to Alice's back. He pulled a tasty treat from his utility belt. Tawanga, a type of dried fruit and fried bugs shaped into chewy sticks that he'd picked up on his travels, had quickly become Alice's favorite snack.

Daniel peered up at the hole in the side of the wreck, which sat two or three floors up. An easy jump with his Aegis, if only he knew what he would be jumping into.

Jasper had the same concern. Protectively blocking Daniel's way with his flipper, he opened his beak and shot a grappling hook up to the branch nearest the opening. The whir of a tiny motor was the only sound the anatom made as he respooled the microwire line and rose up into the air, mouth first.

Dangling in front of the hole, Jasper shone a light inside.

"What do you see?" Daniel called up, which was dumb, because no matter what Jasper saw he couldn't tell Daniel about it. He couldn't talk! "Never mind . . . !"

Jasper swung back and forth for a moment, building momentum until–*click!* He disengaged the grappling hook and leapt into the dark.

A loud clank echoed out from the opening. Followed by more clanks, a squawk, and a couple of bat-like things flying off to find a new home.

Moments later an F-light went on.

Then Jasper's familiar humming started up again.

"I guess that means it's okay," Daniel said, heading back

to Alice to retrieve his backpack. He gave the Hammertail a scratch around the ear. "Don't wander off. I'm going to need you."

Daniel turned back, took a running jump, and–

Whompff!!!

Daniel's Aegis burst into action, creating a controlled wave of iridescent energy that propelled him up and into the opening ripped into the side of the *Coldstar.*

He'd gotten good at controlling this thing.

Daniel landed on one knee and scrutinized his surroundings.

The metal hexagons on his Truth Seeker uniform glinted in the dim light.

A short maintenance passage of some type stretched out before him. The buckled floor had weeds growing up through the grilles. At one time this floor had been the ceiling, but with the ship on its back everything was upside down. Pipes lined either side of the passageway leading down to a heavy pressure door where Jasper was already tinkering with the mechanism to get it to open.

"Stand back," Daniel ordered.

Jasper shook his flippers, trying to indicate that he almost had it, but Daniel didn't feel like waiting. The anatom searched for cover while Daniel reached out his hand. His Aegis swirled, generating a power blast that crushed the lock. The door shook and creaked before sliding open.

Daniel activated his own F-light and tossed it into the

area beyond. He didn't really know what to expect . . .

. . . but this wasn't it: An opulent-looking hallway, wide and deep, ran perpendicular to the maintenance passage. Thick carpet lined the ceiling. It had rotted now, and hung down in sheets like the creepers outside. It must have looked magnificent back in the day when it used to be the floor. Ornate golden patterns lined the walls, and pictures hung at steady intervals along an endless line of doorways, each one marked with a number.

"What kind of ship is this?" Daniel wondered. It reminded him of the hotel in Loronoh, Oota Mheen's capital city, where the Truth Seekers had set up a temporary headquarters for the impending invasion. "This isn't a military vessel," he said. "This is a passenger ship."

Other than the name *Coldstar*, what was his connection to this starliner? The questions multiplied. Why had it crashed? Why did somebody want him to come here and see it? Who was that somebody?

Daniel beckoned to Jasper to keep up. "Come on. We need to find the bridge," he said, leaping down onto what had once been the ceiling.

Jasper waddled along the vertical wall as though it were the most normal thing in the world to do, humming an oddly cheerful little song.

"We're looking for the databanks," Daniel explained, assuming that that was what the penguin wanted to know. "If they're intact, they're my best hope of finding some answers. Think you can copy the data from them?"

Jasper made a rude grunting noise and shook his head.

"Well, why not?"

The anatom ceased his hum and switched to some tuneless funeral dirge.

"Can we at least retrieve them?"

Jasper shrugged. *Maybe.*

Daniel glanced around, trying to get a sense of the layout. "Any idea where the bridge is from here?"

Jasper looked for an answer, zeroing in on a data port halfway up the wall. His yellow light-wire crest glowed briefly as each feather extended out into the receptacle, probing for a connection. A moment later the light-wire feathers pulsed brightly as the data transfer began, faster and faster until–

Sssnappp!

An arc of electricity zipped out of the port, showering the anatom in a cascade of sparks.

Jasper lost his grip and fell to the ground with a heavy *thud!*

Daniel held out his hands. "Well? Where do we go?"

The flustered penguin shook his head before jabbing a flipper into the air.

They needed to go up.

Which of course meant down if the *Coldstar* had been right side up. It seemed that this class of starliner mounted its command center on the very lowest point of the vessel.

Clink! Clink! Clink! Clink! Clink!

"Hold it!" Daniel warned, listening to what sounded like distant footsteps scurrying around the abandoned wreck not far from where they stood. Animals? People? Hard to say.

"Let's go," Daniel urged quietly, helping Jasper up. "Keep your eyes open. I don't think we're alone in here."

They climbed up through twenty or so mangled decks, before Daniel's utility belt chirped. Someone was trying to call. Reluctantly, he ran his palm through the air, bringing up the holographic display. The call was coming from the Seventh Summit, his home with the Truth Seekers on Orpheus Core.

Nails's image popped up, floating in front of him. As long as he lived, Daniel was pretty sure he would never get used to seeing someone with fingernails for hair.

"I told you not to contact me unless it's an emergency. Anyone could be listening in," Daniel said.

Henegan Rann's face briefly crowded into the picture. Rann, Nails, and Fix Suncharge; they were the only other grubs who had made it out of the relic mines when Daniel and the Truth Seekers had come to rescue them.

"This *is* an emergency," Rann said.

Nails pushed him away. "Do you mind?"

"What's going on?" demanded Daniel.

"Time's up," said Nails.

"The Tarafand invasion force is here?" Daniel quipped.

He knew they were still days away.

"Worse."

"Worse? How can it be worse?"

"They're looking for you."

"*Who* are looking for me?"

"Ionica. Ben. They know you're missing. They're out combing the entire area, searching for you."

Daniel dismissed the news by shifting the image to one side so he could still see where he was going. "We knew that would happen." He glanced down at Jasper. The anatom led the way, gesturing for him to follow. Not far now.

"Disappearing in the middle of a rescue mission to go off on this little adventure was never a good idea," Nails insisted.

"What other chance was I going to get?" Daniel argued. It would have been easy to have listened to them back at the Seventh Summit and forgotten about this whole risky venture, but that wasn't who Daniel was. If it had been, he never would have escaped the relic mines in the first place.

"Well, guess what?" Daniel said. "I found it."

Surprise drifted across Nails's face like a sun sliding out from behind a cloud. "Are you serious? It's *real*?"

"Yes, it's real. It's right where he said it would be–"

"*Who* said it would be there?" An angry voice cut in.

Everyone froze.

Busted.